D0421921

# FIVE REHEARSALS

# FIVE
# REHEARSALS

*Susanna Johnston*

CHATTO & WINDUS

THE HOGARTH PRESS

LONDON

Published in 1984 by
Chatto & Windus · The Hogarth Press
40 William IV Street
London WC2N 4DF

British Library Cataloguing in Publication Data
Johnston, Susanna, 1935–
Five rehearsals.
I. Title
823'.914 [F] PR6060.04/

ISBN 0–7011–2840–2

The lines from 'Wild Oats'
from *The Whitsun Weddings* by Philip Larkin
are reproduced by kind permission of
the author and Faber and Faber Ltd.

Typeset at The Spartan Press Limited,
Lymington Hants
Printed in Great Britain by
Redwood Burn Ltd
Trowbridge, Wiltshire

*To Mic Cheetham*

This is a novel,
and the characters in it are fictional.
It is not an autobiography.
I have, occasionally, used incidents from my own life
as a peg on which to hang the plot.
The characters of Vanessa and Johann
are the product of my imagination,
not my life.

S. J.

# Chapter
## I

In spite of the winter weather, Vanessa had taken her uncle to the Wild Life Park. Rhinos, hides eroded, sheltered in huts so the pair could look closely at them from a parapet above and watch the sparrows take refuge in the recesses in their skin.

There was a message waiting for her when she got home. A German gentleman had rung from Hamburg enquiring about a house she owned in Tuscany. It seemed that he wanted to rent it and that he expected her to ring him back. Long distance. Vanessa had never heard his name, but Uncle Jim said it sounded familiar.

'I think he's a film producer, darling. If he's the one I'm thinking of he was married to the daughter of a friend of mine. She's dead, I believe. They say he was foul to her. Don't touch him with a barge-pole.'

'I'll ask a whopping rent.'

'Why not try? It can't be easy to let that house in winter. So damp and dark. Sting him for it.'

She rang the Hamburg number and asked for Johann Kraesel. He sounded knowing. Very familiar with the Tuscan neighbourhood, he was, and ready to point out that she would have few other chances of letting her damp dark house out of season. He needed to concentrate on a film script and wanted somewhere quiet in which to spend three weeks with a colleague. He had been under the weather, and the house should be well aired. All this at her expense. What about central heating, firewood and so on? His English was perfect.

'Could you let me put in a word if I'm to go on paying for this call?' she asked.

'I'm in a hurry. Call me back in the morning. Not too early. I'm celebrating tonight.'

She wasn't having that. 'Think it over and ring me yourself.'

Vanessa needed some money, and tossed about that night fretting over the manners of the stranger.

At eleven o'clock next day he rang her again. He was feeling ropy and more in need than ever to get away with his colleague.

'Yes,' he said. 'I'll take it. I haven't even seen it. Count yourself one of the lucky ones.'

'The rent. I'll have to ask a hundred pounds a week. I ask two fifty in the summer months.'

'Do you want to make me laugh? Who else would take it? A rotten little house like that. A rotten little house on a hillside in winter. Are you a crook?'

Vanessa was a few pounds out of pocket as a result of the film producer, as he turned out to be, from Hamburg. Soon she forgot about him.

Uncle Jim took her to the Barry Humphries show a week later in London. He had been careful not to reserve seats in any of the front rows.

'Can't face the audience participation. It can get so obscene, darling.'

They were in Row M. The star was sporting an outsize penis crammed into khaki shorts.

'There's your film producer sitting in front of you,' her uncle whispered. 'He clearly didn't find a Tuscan hideout rent free. He's the one that married poor Myra. I can't remember the ins and outs but he did filthy things to her, I'm told.'

Van took a good look, happy to rest her eyes from the hitching of the giant member on stage. He was with a handsome girl in a beige hacking-jacket; probably the colleague he had planned to take to Tuscany. He was extraordinary looking. It was hard to say, but he might have been fifty. His head was bony and his dark hair, peppered with silver, close-cropped. His eyes were small, black, bright and incessantly in motion. His lips were flabby and colourless and his nose was hooked. In spite of the coarseness of his features, there was a compelling ferocity about him that arrested her. At a glance Van judged him to be rather drunk. For a second she was perturbed. He might see and recognise her; then she remembered that they had never met. Assured of its irresistibility, he was giving a sidelong leer at the hacking-jacketed companion.

'Do you want to be introduced? I'd forgotten he was a snip-cock.' Uncle Jim always thought of everything.

'Heavens no! What a terrible expression. Let me keep him under observation.'

Uncle Jim had forgotten, too, that Mr Kraesel looked so sexy.

'A real dish.'

He couldn't understand, he said, why Myra had objected to the filthy things.

'She was rather feeble, now I come to think of it. Poor Myra.'

Van forgot about him once again.

In the summer Vanessa drove with her two daughters, Melissa and Polly, to her Italian house. Uncle Jim followed by aeroplane, allowing time for them to settle in. The house was faultless in July and August when the sun beat down from above, and it was hard to remember that it ever had off moments. She thought of the Hamburg telephone calls and became indignant. Fancy expecting to spend three weeks here with that handsome girl for next to nothing. The little property was very sweet. The house was built into the hill and encircled by pine woods. All around were streams, olive trees, and birds, in spite of the mercilessness of the hunters. The drive to the house, and the paths spreading from it into pine woods, were littered with empty cartridges.

Sometimes a kingfisher came, in very hot weather, and once or twice a hoopoe. Uncle Jim helped Vanessa to identify the birds by their calls, as often they were too wary to come near.

They had fun every day swimming in the shabby pool and eating at a rotting table under a heavy Virginia creeper. Van had meant to plant a vine, but her Italian had been bad in the early days and the order had been muddled. Mice had eaten a hammock, the inside of a sofa and two tents during the winter months, and the house looked dilapidated.

Melissa was fifteen; Polly two years younger. Their father had been dead for nine years and Vanessa's refusal to speak of him made the girls fearful, sometimes, of what sort of man he had been. They were good girls and left her in peace on the topic. In all other ways the three of them stuck very close.

At the start of each Tuscan summer they would hasten to visit favourite haunts. A pizzeria in the next village was top of their list. A neon sign, winking green, perched on a tangle of ivy above tables lodged on a slant. Motorbikes shot past; well-brushed Italian heads, defenceless without helmets. This year Lina, the proprietress, charged down the steps, wiping sweat from her face. A scar, sharp and red, ran from the outer corner of her eye and descended in a wiggle to her lip.

'I am ruined,' she wailed, patting puffy clouds of flour from her apron.

'A drunk; an *ubriaco*, threw a glass at me.' She tightened her lips, proud, and pressed fingers to thumbs.

'He was drunk. *Ubriachissimo*. I wouldn't serve him. Now, look at me. I am ruined.'

Lina's face, square and well-composed, meant much to her.

Van, Melissa, Polly and Uncle Jim grouped themselves around the outdoor table and waited for knives and forks which would bend double at the slightest pressure. 'Yuri Gellers', Polly called them.

Lina's husband – also scarred, but from birth: a mushroomy excrescence weighing down half his face – plonked a carafe, netted in plastic wicker, before them. Uncle Jim looked pained. The ordering began.

Combinations had to be sorted out. With or without anchovies. *Senza o con* – olives, rosemary, *prosciutto* or what? They waited as Lina kneaded at pizza dough. She shoved the mixture into a furnace in the wall, twisting it about with a long-handled broom.

Melissa said, 'This is what we come for, isn't it Mum?'

Polly straightened out her fork.

Van said, 'I do love you both.'

Uncle Jim said, 'And I worship you all.'

On the way home, Polly screamed. A cat, wet and weary, dragged itself across the road. Van manoeuvred a skilful swerve, wrenching the wheels. Both girls said, 'Mum. You're fantastic.' They got out. The cat, weighed down with stones, huddled into the verge. A heavy bag hung from under its neck. The head was bowed, tilting sideways; fur soaking wet. It had crawled from a ditch, defeating assassins.

All four of them were kneeling, stretching towards the petrified animal. It had slunk under the car, sideways, dragging its tilting head. Water, dripping from its fur, was tinged with blood. The string round the neck must have cut deep. Each of them extended hands towards it, determined to free it, but the animal, vicious with fear, forced them to abandon their efforts. Polly cried. Driving, unwillingly, at the slowest possible pace, Van, taking instructions from her daughters, avoided brushing it with the car wheels as she left it behind her on the road.

Next day they returned to find it dead. Uncle Jim stayed behind, hoping to read his book.

At a garage on the main road leading to Lucca, Van stopped beside an emblem, an inflated rubber ladybird, and filled the car with petrol. There was a baby there; the grandson of the proprietor, strapped into an upright perambulator beside the pump, under a spotted parasol attached to the hood of his throne. Kicking out with brown legs, rolling black eyes, he was the shiniest thing they had ever seen.

'Hurry on, Mum. You might nick him and then we'd be for it,' Melissa warned.

Then into the town, under ramparts and across the *fosso*, a slimy canal, narrow between brick walls. Leaving the car, they walked towards the centre past a pet shop selling terrapins and a parrot talking Italian. The girls insisted on stopping outside the orthopaedic shop. An entire window was dense with dummies wearing jock-straps designed for hernia sufferers, built-up shoes, false breasts and crepe stockings under a flickering sign, 'Busti e Corsetti Ortopedici'.

Van was untroubled and at ease.

At the house you could always hear visitors walking up the steep and hazardous driveway by their puffing complaints. One of the children would look over the wall bordering the terrace and break the news. On this occasion Polly said:

'Gosh. It's a spooky stranger. He looks a bit creepy.'

He was taller than Van expected and had to bend as he walked towards her from under a low-branched fig tree. Once again she felt the tug of his curious sex appeal.

'Johann Kraesel. I have come to view the spot I was so nearly rooked for. My God!' he said. 'What a hole! I should like a swim and a drink. Then, I think, I shall have had enough.'

'First, you lousy bugger,' she said, 'I want ten thousand lire for that unspeakably unpleasant telephone call I made to Hamburg. You can swim for a hundred pounds and a drink will cost you another hundred.'

'What do I have to pay in order to be allowed to kiss you? You are fat. You are quite old. Your dress is dirty. I suppose you will rook me for a kiss as well.'

Van's children offered their services for large sums and Polly ran to throw water over him from an upstair window. His greying black hair was thick, and it was a moment before he noticed that he was being showered upon. Uncle Jim had been lying down hoping to get forty winks. He looked out of the window, donning his specs.

'I'll offer my services free,' he said. 'I told you he was a dish.' The dish was soaked and writhing.

Kraesel's mastery of the English language was first-class. His flabby mouth drooped open showing large tobacco-stained teeth.

'Who's the Bertie Woofter? I've seen him somewhere before. My God. You English. It's a madhouse.'

Van was wearing red sandals with very high heels. She ran at him and kicked him again and again in the shin. He fell and rolled over, clutching his wounded leg.

'Fuck. I'm maimed for life.'

Van retreated to her semi-darkened bedroom. The light from outside was blocked by an apple tree and pines beyond. She howled and clasped a roll of fat beneath her bosom with both hands and made it wobble. Her blue dress was grubby.

The German walked into her room without warning and sat beside her on the bed. The mattress had never fitted that bed properly and it started to slip with the extra weight. He touched her cheek with the knuckle of a forefinger, brushing away penitential tears. He did this very gently and she knew that calamity had struck.

That evening at the rotting table they ate a huge dinner, starting with rabbit fried in hot oil. Van told the girls that it was chicken and they were taken in.

'Quite honestly, darling,' said Uncle Jim, 'he's not worth much, however dishy. No wonder poor Myra . . .'

'Awful. Perfectly awful. Where can he be staying?'

The young were excited. Polly hugged her mother. She was a hot-blooded child; craving kisses.

'You must admit, Mum, that it was fun. Especially the kicking bit. He's got bedroom eyes. Did he follow you upstairs to apologise?'

Uncle Jim brought out a tray covered in fig leaves and piled high with peaches. Van took one and, biting it, resolved to eat nothing but peaches for weeks and weeks, until those globose rolls under her bosom disappeared.

They drank very cold, very pure, light white wine and water from a spring behind the shed.

In the morning they went to Lucca in the baking sun, some to sight-see, some to try on shoes, and some to use the public telephone. They made a rendezvous at the Bar delle Mura. This, a bar in the noisy corner of the Piazza Napoleone, had caused a recent stir. It belonged to a local baron with puffy hands and Papal connections who liked to amuse himself collecting 'ventures'. He had bought it lock, stock and barrel with its clientele and lissom bar-boys whom he fancied no end. A few months before it had been raided and found to be the centre of vice and drug-smuggling, earning the peaceful city its nickname 'Filthy Lucca'. A great joke among the local English. The Lucchesi Inglesi. An unsophisticated lot.

Slowly the group drew together: Uncle Jim with a bundle of outdated English newspapers and a bag of presents ('Might come in handy'); the daughters with news of the outside world after sessions at the telephone box; Van with bulbs and batteries and a new frock – loose-fitting and synthetic, but clean. Drinks were brought to them under the awning by plump ladies. The lissom bar-boys had been liquidated in a clean-up after the raid.

Johann appeared and, appropriating one of Uncle Jim's newspapers, said: 'May I join you? My leg is bandaged and throbbing.'

The arrow was well shot. Van should have put her new frock on and bundled up the grubby one. She petted Polly and looked down, sipped her drink and ignored him. Johann was a little tipsy but today he was in a merry mood. He pulled a plastic chair away from the next table and moved it into a gap beside Van.

'I give you my address,' he said. 'Also I am on the telephone. You will, please, come to pay me a call. It is not far. My house is high and has a magnificent outlook. I will now pay for your drinks.'

He limped away with Uncle Jim's newspapers.

They left the town, driving through an archway and three villages, then off, to the right, away from the main road and up into the hills. Up her perilous driveway which lay between a ditch and a precipice. They ate their lunch. Meat rissoles with lemon squeezed over them and tomato salad sprinkled with chopped basil. Van ate a peach. It was all very easy. They swam and read and lay in the sun. Uncle Jim tried, once again, to get his forty winks.

Van slipped out after washing her hair and buttoning herself into the new frock. Earlier she had run back to change her shoes, not wanting Johann to be reminded of the red ones that had administered the kicks. It was horrifyingly agitating and difficult to decide whether to ring him first or whether to appear, as he had done the day before, unheralded.

The prospect of telephoning him appalled her, but she remembered the girl he had been with at the theatre. Like a Nazi, she had looked. A tall, beige, beautiful, smiling Nazi in a hacking-jacket. Van pictured the hardening of that smile if caught unawares. She didn't remember the girl's eyes but began to see them as green and glinting, unprotected by lashes. The teeth, she knew for certain, were white and even. What if she were there?

The house was easy to find. She arrived without having faced the decision of whether or not she should telephone. Above her she saw the cemetery behind a grey wall which edged the narrow road. The house was opposite this, looking down upon the valley and commanding, as Kraesel had boasted, a magnificent outlook. She left her car in the dusty yard by the cemetery and crossed the road to a small archway crawling with lizards. There was a dark lady dressed in black. Perhaps she had recently deposited one of her nearest in the graveyard opposite. Van asked for the *tedesco*, hoping not to be mistaken for one herself. The bereaved-looking lady smiled sweetly. The smile convinced Van that Johann was alone. The lady, she was sure, would have been anxious were one woman to surprise him with another.

Opening the door, she saw a dark, steep staircase. The bottom step was partly covered by a squatting toad. Contemplating kissing it on the lips, Van stooped down to meet its face. Perhaps it would change into a prince and save her a lot of bother. With the wet coldness of the toad near her hot dry face, she changed her mind. Her cheek would burn into it and she had always dreaded hurting any animal, even a wasp. She went on up and, opening a low door at the top of the flight, appeared in a ravishing sitting-room. She couldn't exactly understand the house, what floor she was on or where she was facing, but she was entranced by the look of it. It was bursting with faded furniture, silver mirrors, lace and tattered rugs. From the corner of the room, disturbing the peace, came the loud noise of ham fists on a typewriter and the sound of Johann saying 'Fuck!'

To her horror he was wearing a Japanese kimono and floppy sandals.

He looked delighted. Leaving his typewriter, he hobbled towards her and kissed her on the lips.

'Come and sit down.' They sat beside one another on an exquisite wooden-framed sofa. Very uncomfortable.

'I have been typing all day and my fingers are stiff. Please massage my knuckles.' He looked at Van appealingly and she saw what Polly had meant about the eyes.

'Please my sweet,' he said again, putting his hand on her knee. She might have been a manicurist. There seemed to be no way out so, gingerly, she began to rub.

'Harder. Harder.'

Then she let him have it, screwing his fingers off.

'Wonderful wonderful. Go on. My day will be complete.'

She wasn't sure about her own day but enjoyed the sensation of his squirming.

'Now, my darling, my toes.'

'Have you been typing with your toes?'

'Very funny. Very funny. Please my sweet.'

She was down on the floor manipulating his toes and longing for him to make love to her. It was difficult to drop a hint with him sitting there, wriggling with delight. She would have to bide her time. Her moment came.

'Upstairs,' he said. He pulled her hair gently and touched her cheek again.

'Now,' he said, when they were side by side on a four-poster bed festooned with mosquito nets of filmy whiteness.

'Now, my dearest, I would like to be squeezed, very gently, all over. Omit, of course, the portion of my leg which is bandaged and still throbbing. Pretend that I am a toothpaste tube. Start at the bottom and work your way up. Would that you could split my chest open with a knife and rip all impurities from it. Stroke my arm. Very gently. Wonderful.'

She persuaded him to make love.

'Now,' he said, 'I am tired. I will take two valiums and a mogadon. You must leave me. I can never sleep with another person in the room. I am short of sleep. That is one of the problems. That and the throbbing.' '

He spoke with a plum in his mouth. Maybe, at some stage, he had been instructed in elocution. He reached out for a flat box with a transparent lid, like a bead box, neatly divided into compartments. Each compartment held different coloured pills.

'What are they all for?'

'Sleeping, calming, restoring, throbbing, sexual potency. That sort of thing.'

Enraged, she turned on him. 'With me in your bed you should be taking dexedrine. Not valium and sleeping pills. It's hideously insulting.'

'You would understand if you knew what it was to be short of sleep. If I can't sleep I can't write and that is a disaster. Come back tomorrow.'

'I can't. I have to take Uncle Jim to Pisa airport.'

'Pisa airport! Be an angel and get me some newspapers. English, American, German. As many as possible. I'll pay you back. Bring them in the evening. Now I must sleep.'

Nobody seemed to have noticed her absence. Uncle Jim had had his forty winks and was busying himself with packing.

'I can't bear leaving you like this. Promise not to let that ghastly Hun trouble you.'

She was sorry to see her uncle go. He was already in another world wearing his tidy suit. Once he had disappeared, following the queue, into the departure area, she walked quickly to the airport shop. The pile of newspapers she bought weighed her down. In the tunnel that cuts through the Pisan hills, she planned the evening before her. She would give the girls a wonderful dinner. Butterfly-shaped pasta, perhaps, with an enticing sauce. Their tastes and enthusiasms were still child-like. She wouldn't con them over rabbit again. It would be a little early, then she would slither away.

'Boring drinks with those Americans. I have to do it once a year and I couldn't have inflicted it on Uncle Jim. He met them once and couldn't bear them. Something to do with names on matchboxes.'

Apart from the occasional white lie over menus, Van had never deceived her girls before. They had always worked as a unit.

She stuck to her plan and once again parked her car by the cemetery. The toad had gone. She went up the dark stairway and emerged in the enchanting room. The typewriter was silent and there was nobody about. Putting the pile of newspapers down on the sofa where she had rubbed his toes and fingers the day before, she called his name. It was the first time she had done this and it gave her a fright.

'I'm in the bath,' he shouted. 'Come and wash my back.'

His back was magnificent. Smooth and young and plump. This was unexpected considering the lanky skinniness of his frame.

'I've brought some papers.'

'Wonderful woman. Wonderful and beautiful.'

'Old and fat too, perhaps?'

'Yes. That too, but very beautiful. That is why I wished to meet you.'

She wanted to find out more.

He asked her if she would like something to eat. She had already eaten, she said, not telling him that it had been one peach.

'I shall make myself an omelette. Have you ever eaten one of my omelettes?'

'How on earth could I have eaten one of your omelettes?'

'Sorry. I am forgetful. I shall make one this evening with sorrel. Finely chopped sorrel from the hill.'

Not understanding what she said, Van told him that it was a vulgar affectation to talk about herbs.

'In that case you will be hearing more four-letter words from me. Basil, thyme, lovage, angelica.'

It seemed to her that he made rather a song and dance about

his omelette, whisking and beating and tasting. But she was used to cooking, having reared a family. He ate ferociously and then remembered about the newspapers.

'Bliss. What bliss. I want to kiss you.' He enfolded her in his kimono and then fell upon the newspapers. He remained, reading them, on the pretty sofa for an hour or more.

Forgetting that she had eaten nothing but peaches for several meals now, Van poured herself a glass of wine and walked onto the terrace. The air was full of the smell of herbs. 'Four letter words,' she said aloud. Her stomach was empty and so, now, was her glass. She went to the corner of the sitting-room where the wine was kept. Johann didn't notice her or stir.

After finishing her second glass on the terrace, she felt rather drunk and terribly cross. She pulled the paper away from him and sat down on his knee, crushing the kimono.

'How old are you anyway? Are you a widower? Who was that Nazi you took to the Barry Humphries Show? Why did you ring me from Hamburg pretending you wanted to rent my house, insulting and unsettling me?'

He was shaken.

'I am fifty-two. You are hurting my wounded leg. Yes. Myra is no longer alive. The lady I took to the Barry Humphries Show? What are you talking about? Well. You wouldn't know her. An ex-girlfriend of mine. I mean ex. Why did I ring you? That we will talk about later. I met you once. You don't remember. You paid no attention to me whatsoever. I had to do it differently. That's all.'

'Do you want to be my friend?'

'Very much.'

'Is that official? Are we now officially friends?'

'It is a fact.'

'Did you sleep after I left you yesterday afternoon? Did those pills do their job?'

'They did but I have limited powers of recovery. I am still very tired.' They were back in the veil of mosquito netting.

'Please tell me about that girl. The one in the beige hacking-jacket.'

'What are you saying? How do you know what she wore?'

'I sat behind you. Row M. You didn't pay much attention to me that evening so we are even.'

'Strange woman. Beautiful. I love you madly. My darling. Go and fetch me a glass of whisky. Whisky and a little water. Run the water very cold.'

Off she went to the bottle and the tap. She let the tap run for a bit but the water didn't come out very cold. She squeezed a lump of ice from a plastic container in the freezer and plopped it into the glass, carried it to his side of the bed and, brushing aside the netting, held it to his mouth.

'Christ. I never asked for ice. Now you have ruined it. You must start again.'

She did everything he asked. She squeezed him like a toothpaste tube and massaged his toes. She brought him drinks until he was insensible and then she stole away. Driving up her hill, through an avenue of pollarded limes, she was happy as never before.

A charm was at work on her. She dwelt on the rash discovery of a new sensation, indifferent now to exercising the slightest self-restraint.

When she woke, the next day, she realised that they had made no further date to meet. She couldn't call on him unexpectedly again. It frightened her too much. She would have to wait.

Melissa and Polly were often out. Both girls had good looks and attracted a crowd. They had spoken Italian from the word go and were besieged with invitations from handsome lads in the neighbourhood. In the evenings Fernandos, Luigis and Stefanos by the score would drive them to the sea, and often to a roller-skating rink. Sometimes Van was alone with nobody to cook for, particularly now that she was only eating peaches. The roll of fat was disappearing. She was feeling forgotten bones and wanting Johann to feel them too. She sat on the stone table outside the kitchen swinging her legs for exercise and devising plots.

Having neglected her neighbours during Uncle Jim's visit, it came to her that she should call on Brigid, an English woman living all alone in a large farmhouse high in the hills the other side of the town. She had been the original contact with Johann, the one who put him in touch with her.

Driving up the twisty road to Brigid's house through chestnut woods and vineyards, she had to brake suddenly. A fat fox ran over the road in front of her. Her heart turned over as it always did when she saw a fox. The lady at the post office had told her that they came out for the grapes at this time of year. This had amused her, believing, until then, that such things only happened in fables.

Brigid was alone.

'You must stay and have supper with me. We will eat on the terrace. Pot luck you know, but plenty of wine. I sit up here alone most of the time drinking and dreaming of lost love.'

She was tall and elegant. Possibly in her sixties, her face unlined and her eyes bright.

'I hope you didn't mind me giving your number to Johann Kraesel. He was going to London and wanted to see you. He's an odd fish.'

'He wanted to rent my house but I believe he took another one. I asked too much for it.'

'How come he wanted to rent your house? He has his own out here. It belonged to his wife, poor dear. Myra. She was half Italian and inherited it from her father. It's a delightful place – full of pretty things. Four-poster beds and suchlike.'

Van was astonished. She'd assumed the house to be a rented one and had intended to ask Johann about its owner. There hadn't been an appropriate moment and he was not an easy man to question.

'Perhaps he was enquiring for a friend. He didn't follow it up.'

'Maybe. It's good to see you. You've lost weight. Aren't you beautiful.'

'Tell me more about that man.'

'He spends most of his time in Hamburg. He's a film director and a script-writer. Quite successful. He told me that he had seen you at the film festival in Lucca last year and that he had been struck with you.'

Van thought back to that concert and realised now, by strange chance, she had not sighted him there.

Brigid told Van that her niece had moved into a little house at the foot of the garden with her husband, Michael. They were there indefinitely with a small child. It didn't seem to be working out.

'Even the cats look unhappy in that house. One of them had a broken tail and trails it up and down the stairs. Michael fiddles with his mobiles and does nothing to help Carola. They have no money, so I let them live here. We'll call on them after supper. Perhaps you could ask them over one evening and try to cheer them up?'

Van liked this idea.

Brigid said, 'Their marriage has been on the rocks and they're trying to put it together. It doesn't seem hopeful. Something's wrong.'

Together they went to the little house. It looked dejected. The cat with the broken tail was scratching at a toy in a heap of sand beside the front door. Michael invited them in with a bad grace. Carola, he said, had popped down to the village and Charlotte, the little girl, was asleep. The room was a muddle, things all over the floor. He poured out some wine and waved his hand to the terrace where giant sunflowers looked tipsily in at them.

'Shall we sit outside? It's a mess in here.'

They sat among the sunflowers looking down at a blackened field and singed olive trees. It had been a dry summer and there had been alarming forest fires in the neighbourhood. Van thought thankfully of the springs and streams that rippled on her side of the mountain.

'I'm trying to construct a mobile,' Michael said, 'inspired by the fire. It could be the best thing I've done.' He talked about his work; how he had been diddled by galleries, dealers and agents. Brigid rolled her eyes.

They heard a voice indoors.

Carola came out to meet them. There she was. She was wearing a cotton trouser suit and her mouse-coloured hair was cut abruptly, very straight, below her shoulders. Her teeth were indeed white and her eyes green and glinting. Van felt panicky and was, once again, in a state of unfounded terror at the thought of being recognised.

A specialist in sham shyness, Carola looked anguished.

'Help,' she said softly. 'Panic. Have you got drinks?' She smiled bewitchingly and looked behind her expecting further surprises. After that she hardly spoke but looked at Van from time to time. She didn't look like a Nazi now, but like an outsize faun.

The next day Johann appeared, bumptious and sun-tanned, on the terrace in front of Vanessa's house. He was not limping and said that he had been waiting to hear from her.

'I can't contact you in this dump without a telephone. Hem, hem. What have you been doing all alone here with those children of yours?'

He took her away with him, promising her lunch in the town. First they had to go to the post office where he bartered and badgered. Postal speeds and prices were amongst his bugbears.

Here Van had a further glimmer of his power-proving ways. Would he have waited with patience whilst she kissed Polly, changed a light fitting or dusted a shelf? Then he had newspapers to buy. The foreign ones had been snapped up which made him swear. He took a copy of *Le Figaro* and led her to a bar in the great central piazza where he ordered a drink for each of them and then settled to a good read. It seemed as though he devoured every sentence on every page.

He handed her a penknife.

'You are so brilliant in every way,' he said. 'Perhaps you could mend this. I'm lost without it. It's really a boy scout's knife. One of the blades has got stuck, the stoutest one. There. Please mend it.' She tinkered with the knife while he read the paper. Then he pulled a dozen or more postcards out of his pocket and began to write on them, very densely, in a spiky foreign hand.

'I met Carola last night,' she told him. She had hoped to look tough but her voice was shrill. At least she put an end to the postcard writing.

'Women are fucking bores. I suppose you got together and turned me into a clown.'

'Not that. She didn't know me. She doesn't know that I know you. We talked of other things. I rather fell for her. She's infinitely seductive.'

'Don't start some dykey thing with Carola. She'd love it. Man, woman or child. Anything would do for Carola. Christ! What a woman. Is she back with Michael? I swore never to see her again after that night I saw you, or rather you saw me, at the theatre.'

In the restaurant Van ate an enormous amount, abandoning her diet. Johann drank quantities of wine, pushing away food.

'You should know by now that I am paranoid. I would like to live in hospital and be looked after by nuns. I cried this morning when I saw a nun. I tell you this in order to explain how sensitive I am. I should like to have a drip attached to my arm. A whisky drip and I would like nuns to wash my private parts. You could come from time to time to massage my body.'

'Thanks a bunch,' she said. They leant across the table to kiss each other's lips.

'I can't allow you to talk to Carola about me. It would enrage me. You must promise.'

That evening Carola came alone. She was agonisingly thin.

'I'm sorry,' she said. 'I'm sure you didn't want me on my own but the others couldn't come and one can't ring you. Charlotte wasn't well so Michael had to stay. Isn't this nice? It's perfect. Lovely. Goodness.'

Carola told Van that things had been very bad.

'It was my fault. I fell in love last year. I couldn't help it. He was an impossible man. Rather wonderful but impossible. He used to fag me.'

'What sort of fagging?'

'Silly things. Buy newspapers and massage his toes.'

Van laughed. She nearly always liked the person she was with. She wanted to pool their experiences, fingers, toes and so on.

Carola said, 'The trouble is that the man in question lives in these parts, at least for some of the year. I believe he's out here at the moment and I keep expecting him to pop up when I'm in the town. And he knows my aunt. She never knew of our affair. He might call on her any day. He doesn't know I'm living here. He hates me now.'

'Are you still in love with him?'

'Nobody ever gets over him. He's impossibly self-obsessed and can barely live with himself, let alone anybody else. He's terribly irritable. Mainly, though, he's irritated by himself.'

All night Van pondered on the conversation she had had with Carola.

Once again she was in bed with Johann. In the bed, she now knew, of his late lamented father-in-law and surrounded by his charming possessions. She ran her fingers over Johann's temples at his request. He reached out for the box with the transparent lid.

'Which are the ones for sexual potency?' she asked.

'These,' he said. 'The green ones. Go and fetch me a glass of whisky. No ice. I will take a handful. Then you will be satisfied.' When she returned with his drink he made believe that his mouth was full of green pills.

'Now,' he warned. 'You might get more than you bargained for.'

Then followed a night which left her in a state of euphoria. It was flattering whatever the circumstances.

She asked him the name of the pills.

'You bloody fool. You are the pills. Now leave me. This time I'm not shamming. Hand me a mogadon and leave me to sleep. I love you madly.'

'And I,' she said, 'want you to sleep well. I'll come tomorrow with a billion newspapers and nuns and anything else you want. Basil, lovage, thyme, anything.'

'Newspapers please, and, my dearest, stamps and more postcards. I send them to women all over Europe to keep myself alive in their memory.' She was nearly sick. After a night like that.

When Van returned the next day, laden with newspapers and weak from the night before, he provided her with a shopping list.

'Go to a good greengrocer,' he instructed. 'Also to a chemist. I need some cotton buds.'

# Chapter
## II

Carola lay heavily on her bed, her face hidden in the grey pillow-case, dreading any interruption. She lay there, hating them all, her husband, her aunt and her little daughter. Also that woman she had confided in the night before. She must have been drunk. Normally she kept her secrets, mingily, to herself.

Hers was a horrid little house. Dusty and dark. She had let things get into a state. The kitchen was bad and she hadn't tackled the problem of rubbish. Nobody collected refuse from that remote spot. The melancholy cats dealt with rats and mice. There were two or three buckets containing Michael's and Charlotte's dirty clothes. She wasn't going to wash them. She felt heavier and heavier. It was impossible to move. Michael had been foul since their reunion. He should have fussed over her and realised how lucky he was to have her back. It should now be them, the two of them, against the world. Instead of this he seemed to hanker after society and to be bored with her alone on the side of a burnt-out mountain. He tinkered with little bits of wire all day and appeared to be resigned, listening to taped music and occasionally fixing himself a snack. Now he was gazing at that blackened view. He expected her to wash and iron and take Charlotte for walks. She would have to take a line. She had left him briefly and had returned. Should he not be grateful? Even little Charlotte, at four years of age, didn't realise that it was her mother's prerogative to be difficult. Then there was the question of her looks. Were they beginning to fade? She was over thirty and things would go from bad to worse. Why had she told that woman that she was still in love with Johann? Thank heavens she had not told her who he was.

Carola dragged herself up and looked in the mirror. Normally this was the one positive action capable of restoring her spirits. Today she wasn't sure. Beautiful, of course. She was particularly pleased by the line of her cheek bones. Something would have to be done. She took a silk frock from a heap on a chair in the corner of her bedroom and ironed it with spirit. Michael could see to Charlotte when she returned with her great-aunt from an outing in the town. Carola detested Brigid, but was not proof against enlisting her services in a spurious crisis.

Carola needed distraction. That was why she'd gone to see that smug middle-aged woman the night before. So self-satisfied she had been, protected by teenage daughters, cooking wonderfully and talking about the garden. So respectable to be a widow. She would go to Johann's house, twenty miles off, for a reconnoitre. He had vowed never to see her again but she decided to ignore him.

Climbing the stairway towards the sitting-room, she thought she heard voices. She stopped to listen. Certainly there were, but she couldn't detect how many. The room was empty. The voices came from the kitchen. Johann was up to his cooking tricks again, talking about mozzarella and parmigiano. Basil and thyme. She walked in to find him, in the same old kimono by the sink, squeezing the juice from a fat tomato. Van sat by the kitchen table laughing at him.

'Goodness you do make an opera out of your cooking.'

'Hello.'

'Hem, hem,' said Johann. 'Have you two met?'

He kissed Carola's face. Carola thanked her lucky stars that she had not given away the identity of her lover.

'I am preparing for company. Mrs Langford has arrived early and is kindly assisting me with preparations. Please join us. I will lay another place.'

'No. I'll go.' Her smile was angelic.

Johann looked dismayed. He let the fat tomato splosh onto the draining-board and turned towards the unexpected visitor. His flabby bottom lip dropped and his black eyes shot from side to side of each socket. Now he didn't leer, but his open mouth betrayed the suspicion of a snarl.

'You'd better stay.' He told her. He scooped the tomato from the board and ordered the women out.

'I must concentrate on the sauce. You girls go and have a drink in the other room. I need peace for this job. See to the arrivals. Stay, both of you, for Christ's sake.' He started to sing in a powerful baritone voice.

The women sat, side by side, on the pretty sofa.

'Do you know Mrs Masterman?' Van asked. 'This is for her, this dinner. Apparently she always comes to Florence at this time of year.'

Carola looked grumpy and made no reply.

Mrs Masterman emerged from the dark stairway.

'Isn't this bliss?'

She was over seventy and unpleasant to look at. Her dress was close-fitting and shiny, covered with a floral pattern of bright colours. Her eyebrows were neatly plucked and her lips coated with red gloss. Her car and chauffeur had been left, alongside Van's and Carola's, in the dusty yard by the cemetery.

'Do you know,' she announced, when Johann joined them, 'there is nowhere in the world that I would rather be at this moment in time than in this ravishing drawing-room and in this stimulating company. The sound of the frogs outside and that blissful smell of crushed herbs. No, don't tell me. I really am in Tuscany. Pretty women, Johann. Trust you. Pretty women and the smell of country cooking.'

Johann said 'Hem, hem. We're having your favourite pudding. Peach ice-cream. As you know there is a peach orchard below and at this time of year . . .'

'Don't tell me. It's too much . . .' The other women looked at each other.

Two men appeared as if through a hatch. 'Bertie Woofters, I do declare,' thought Van. How awful Johann's expressions were. Greetings were exchanged.

Van knew that there was only one thing at stake. Which of them was going to stick it out, and be the last to leave? That was all that mattered. It mattered very much. She would stay for ever, until she won.

This she did after a fashion.

She became very drunk half way through dinner. Carola remained cool and sat there, unnerving Johann, as Mrs Masterman continued to extol the charms of Tuscan life.

Van tottered away and, parting the mosquito nets, slipped into a torpor in the father-in-law's bed.

Her gums ached and her teeth felt loose in their sockets as she groped her way down the staircase. Her feet were a long way away and there was no concentration in her as she opened the door of her car by the cemetery. Just deep misery. She was cheered to find a letter from Uncle Jim on her bed when she reached home as dawn broke.

'I loved my time with you as always,' he wrote. 'I do pray that the kraut hasn't turned up again. I've been doing a bit of research and it seems that he is lethal with the ladies. I'm having dinner with Myra's mother tonight. I may not find out much as she's practially ga-ga, poor love. She's taken to pinching everything in sight so nobody can risk having her to their houses. Heigh ho. I shall take her to a restaurant. It can't matter too much if she snitches a wine glass. I'll keep you posted about the kraut. Tear this up in case he comes snooping round and I find myself behind bars. You'd be a lovely prison visitor but I'd sooner see you in the open.'

Before lying down, she hid the letter in a bedside cupboard along with other letters and lay back on her pillow, still dressed in the clothes carefully chosen for the dinner party.

It began to come back to her, painfully and with gaps.

To begin with she had enjoyed the dinner, her enjoyment heightened by panic at Carola's unexpected appearance.

Johann's operatic treatment of the food had been funny. He had whirled around the table in his kimono holding a flaming pan, throwing blackened pancakes onto each plate. The Woofters had looked at each other. They had seen this act before. Carola had cringed and eaten nothing. Van had poured wine into her own glass at a rate of knots. She had talked fast and made the Woofters simper.

Then she was drunk and had made her escape, lurching to the bedroom, shedding clothes. Later she had heard the noise of departures. Mrs Masterman's tones o'ertopping the rest.

'Say farewell to Mrs Langford for me. Has she passed out? How I hate drunken women. Poor Johann. Are you stuck with her for the night? Oh, the noise of the frogs!' In fact there were no frogs in that dry spot, only the occasional toad: but the noise of cicadas, chirping shrilly, was riproaring.

Van had lain still, fearing she would be sick, straining for the sound of Carola's movements.

'We will have to use the other room.' Johann's voice was loud and hard.

'Not the duvet, Johann,' Carola spoke softly. 'I loathe that awful duvet.'

'It is practical and, anyway, I call it a continental quilt.'

How would it have gone if she had remained sober?

She packed to leave three weeks earlier than usual. Melissa and Polly, dismayed at having to break off so abruptly in the middle of their annual Tuscan fun, were brave about it; something was wrong. Never before had they had to share their mother. This year she was slipping away from them. Very sweetly, they agreed to alter the normal pattern and tried to appear happy to return to their pets.

Van could not have remained in the neighbourhood, avoiding the town, the bars, newspaper shops and English-speaking neighbours, jumping out of her skin at each rustle in the driveway.

It was a relief to return to the village in Cambridgeshire where she had lived, first with Martin, her husband, then on her own with the children after Martin's death. She would persuade Uncle Jim to come down and then she would tell him of her adventure.

'Hello love. Wonderful that you're back so soon. So much to

tell. First I must try to recall all I've heard about that awful kraut. Do you remember? The one you kicked?'

She remembered all right. Her heart was in fragments.

She listened, eyes on the fire, as Uncle Jim repeated all he had put together about Johann's earlier life.

He had lived in England since the age of one. The son of a banker, he and his father had escaped from Germany well before the war. His father had smuggled out a small amount of money and joined some other fellow in a plastics business near Slough. He had been interned during the war. Johann's mother, unbelieving, had stayed behind in Germany.

Teased and tormented for his German name; without father or mother, siblings or friends, Johann as a toddler was evacuated to some country mansion, picking up diseases and foul language. There his hypochondria had been born, along with his need to be looked after and his revulsion against caring for others. Later he had gone to university on a scholarship. After his studies he had returned to Hamburg to join an uncle in the film world.

Uncle Jim broke off for a second and looked hard at his niece. Her face was very pink.

Then he went on to tell her that Johann had married Myra twenty-eight years before, when they were both very young.

Myra, half-Italian and half-Hungarian, had been a very skinny beauty. She had a girl friend, also half-Hungarian, who had perfected the technique of mixing powerful unguents for rubbing into the human body, replacing natural oils and so on. She brewed them in brilliant colours, decanted them into old-fashioned chemist's jars and sold them to anybody she could collar.

Myra purchased a complete set, six bottles in all, and perched them, side by side, on the mantelpiece. They caught Johann's eye at once, on his first visit to her after their meeting in a Yugoslavian night club. He asked her what their purpose was and, on being told, developed a craving for Myra to massage these oils into the back of his neck with her lean fingers. The desire became stronger and stronger. There were few lengths to which he would not go in order to achieve his aim. Finally, after weeks of insistent demands, he lay face down on the floor of her little room in the basement of her mother's house, Myra astride, slapping purple oil into his vertebrae. After the long wait Johann was intoxicated, and proposed to her as she rubbed. Although she had not yet taken to thieving, Myra's mother was devilish and pushed her daughter to throw in her lot with the sexy-looking Jewish boy. She was anxious to have Myra off her hands.

Pieces of this story had been winkled out of Myra by her mother, shortly before her daughter's demise, and relayed to Uncle Jim. But Van had heard enough: she stopped her uncle in his tracks.

Uncle Jim, partly responsible for his niece's upbringing, smelt a rat.

'What happened after I left? I know you and your volcanic temperament. Don't say you went and fell for him?'

She confessed it all. The rubbing and the newspapers and even the drunken climax.

'Don't think you've heard the last of him, darling. If his ex-mother-in-law is anything to go by, he'll cling on until he's done you in. For crying out loud, cut him out.' These arbitrary injunctions gave her hope. Perhaps, even after all that, Johann would contact her again.

The following morning there was a letter from him. She recognised the spiky hand, remembering the morning when he had written postcards as she fiddled with the blade of his knife. The envelope was thick and expensive. She hid it from Uncle Jim who was standing nearby as she picked it off the mat. He was waiting for his cup of tea and lightly boiled egg.

'Anything exciting?' he asked. 'And don't forget to hand on the stamps. One of them looked foreign.' He collected stamps for his boy friend. 'Gordon was thrilled with the last lot. We stuck them in while we were eating our pasties and chips.' Van had never been allowed to meet Gordon. She used to worry about their diet and often tried to force fresh vegetables on the menage 'to ward off scurvy' but her uncle said 'no', Gordon liked tins and packets.

The letter said:

Darling.

Where did you go to? I shall be in London next week and hope
to see you. I have done a swap for three months. My house here
will be occupied by an English journalist engaged in writing the
biography of some crappy film-star. In exchange I will use his
house in Kennington. Where the hell is that? We will meet
frequently. Could you supply me with the following: a food
liquidiser, pot plants and a television set. Also I would like you
to book me in at a good health farm. Plenty of massage and
make sure they have what I call the boiled egg: white cabins
filled with steam encasing all but the head. My face needs
attention too so I would like a session with a beautician – face
packs etc. Look after yourself.

All my love, Johann.

He had left her with little time to look after herself.

At the crack of dawn she shaved her legs; each one twice until
they were both as slippery as swansdown. A set of underclothes
lay, new and neat, on a chair. At the very last minute they would
be donned, seconds before departure. Scrubbing at her teeth she
looked, long and close, into the glass. Then she clipped at her
toenails with sharp scissors. These unfolded from a boy scout's
knife, new and red, a replica of the one she had fiddled with at
the bar in Lucca while Johann wrote postcards to women. A
flowered frock, a thing acquired for the occasion, hung in the
sun on the washing line, puffing into billows. It needed fresh air
in and around it to exorcise shoppiness. It was too early for her
hairdresser's appointment. She made tea and drank it without
sugar or milk. Not one calorie would enter her body that day;
not until evening. The new frock was a tight fit. Somebody once,
describing a frock, had said 'It's gaudy but not neat.' What if
that applied to hers? She had little dress sense.

Removing rings, she dropped one hand into a bowl of soapy
water, warm and comforting, while the girl got to work on its

pair, filing and pushing at cuticles. Johann would have relished it. Perhaps he was making preparations. Her hair was washed, then curled, dried, then combed, thick and shiny. It looked great.

A packet of peppermints for the drive was tucked into a compartment in her bag. She would need to smoke and then to clear away the fumes before their first kiss. Before their lips touched at the bar where Johann had arranged for them to meet. Time froze, then flew. Perhaps she would need a nightdress. Packing one, she spoke aloud.

'Pray God I don't have to wear it. Not for a single second.'

She was on her way, smoking, whisking peppermints around the inside of her mouth with her tongue, then smoking again, telling herself to get the order right at the last ditch.

The back of her car rattled with oddments. Bits and pieces he had bidden her bring.

They had arranged to meet at a drinking club in the centre of London. Johann would be there before her. She was carrying a heavy parcel, large and square, secured with a sharp metal binding. This contained a food-liquidiser; a Magimix. A jasmine plant framed to look like a hoop, two pink azaleas and a small winter violet, she had left in the car. Taut with excitement, she rested the heavy parcel on the bonnet of her car as she flicked her hair about with a wire brush. Then she whirled in, rather fast, head held high. He was sitting at a table raised on a platform opposite the bar. He looked at her with rheumy eyes and tugged her face towards his.

'You're here,' he said. 'Sit down and have a drink.' Then he belched loud and long. 'D'you want to go to the cinema?'

He was slipping off his perch. She helped him up and guided him with difficulty down the stairs from the sitting area. Then along a narrow exit route alongside the bar to the kiosk where a pretty girl looked after the coats of clients. Johann tried to kiss the girl as she handed him his new duffle coat and Homburg hat.

In the street he lurched up to a parking meter. Van feared he was going to rape it.

She laughed as she disentangled him. She helped him to climb into her car, then walked around to the driver's seat. As she opened the door he tumbled out onto the road. A Charlie Chaplin film.

This gave her great strength, and before long they were heading for Kennington, Johann insensible and quiescent.

Van spent the evening fixing a plug to the electric food-mill, tending pot plants and having a good look round. It was a nice house, part of a Victorian terrace. A small iron gate opened onto a yard or two of patterned terrazza leading to the front door. Then a narrow passage with the staircase directly in front of it and on the left the door to the main room; straight ahead were three steps down to the kitchen in which there was a door out to a square paved garden. This was a playground for cats. Some of them looked well cared for, as far as Van could see, with only the light from inside the house to guide her. Two of them were even wearing collars. She was pleased that he wouldn't be lonely there. The kitchen was obviously occupied by Johann. A string of garlic hung from the ceiling. A large vat of olive oil, the best from Lucca, and a jam jar bursting with continental parsley, the anaemic wilting type as opposed to the nice, brightly-coloured English variety, took up the corner shelf. A couple of spicy-looking sausages drooped from a nail and a dark, floury loaf sweated on a wire rack.

Johann had baked it himself earlier in the day before his round of tippling began. In the sitting-room there was a collection of filing boxes each labelled on the back in Johann's huge handwriting. One said 'Correspondence'; the others said 'Travel', 'Health' and 'Insurance'. There were bottles of wine, vodka and Perrier water. The television had not yet arrived, although Van had ordered it for the day before. She was vexed and hoped he wouldn't be disappointed by her lapse in efficiency. She crawled into bed beside him at midnight, gingerly so as not to wake him from his sluggish sleep.

She was alert when he awoke, desperate for a glass of water and searching for his pill-box. He had pulled the continental quilt onto his side and she was cold, although it was not yet winter. He had been farting which made her feel at a tremendous advantage. He mauled her vaguely and she noticed that his breath smelt awful. This also made her feel superior. She sprang out of bed to fetch him a glass of water being careful not to put any ice into it. He was swearing when she returned.

'God I loathe my body. I'd like to have it sawn up. Can one have one's body amputated? Pretend that I have just come in on a stretcher and feel each bone for breakages. Start with the toes. Each one gently. Pretend that you are a nurse. I will imagine you to be in uniform. Did you book me into a health farm? I would like to have been a blue baby. Then I could have had my blood changed. Rub me all over when you have fetched me more water. Bring a jug and some ice.'

Off she pattered, struggling with the bursting ice-box. It needed de-frosting. The journalist who was writing the biography of some crappy film-star in Johann's Tuscan house wasn't altogether streamlined. She would have to see to one or two things. He asked her if she knew of a good doctor.

'I'm ill,' he said. 'Have we ever discussed my health?' She told him that they had barely ever strayed from the topic. 'Sorry,' he said, 'I'm confusing you with somebody else.'

In the morning he was as merry as a cricket and brought her a tray in bed.

'Bucks Fizz,' he said, as he tiptoed around the bed. He walked on the balls of his feet, springy and silent. He always walked like that, except when drunk, but Van noticed it for the first time and wondered about it. Perhaps it had some significance. Ready to run in and out of things quickly and quietly maybe. She drank the Bucks Fizz, ate a slice or two of home-made bread and headed for home, after a long loving kiss and a firm dismissal.

'Now I have to work. I'll see you next week. Could you please write to me? I like to get letters. It comforts me to find something in the post.'

He rang her from the health farm.

'Wonderful woman. It's perfect here. Next time I would like you to come with me. I was rubbed all over today by a Burmese child with strong fingers; almost as good as yours. I tried to make her – no – that doesn't matter.' Van encouraged him.

'Stop it. Shut up. I shall have the boiled egg in half an hour and my black-heads squeezed this afternoon. I'm in heaven. You are a wonderful woman. Have I ever told you that before?'

They established a pattern. She would drive to London twice a week and spend these nights with him in Kennington. They would talk to each other on the telephone every day and write letters as often as the gaps in their meetings allowed. Johann loved the squeak of his own pen and wrote endlessly on thick paper, on one side only. For some reason this was the only thing that Van found irritating about him. The rest she adored.

Sometimes, when he was sober, they would go to a concert or play. Sometimes they went to restaurants, and sometimes he would prepare a gourmet dinner at Kennington. Van never enjoyed these dinners as much as she expected. She was prepared for the operatic fashion in which he cooked but hated the long stage-waits and having to comment and applaud so tirelessly.

The nights under the duvet became more and more precious to her with the whining of cats from the patch behind the house and nocturnal demands of every sort from Johann. Three months and more slipped by and there was no talk of his giving the house back.

Uncle Jim warned her that she was riding for a fall.

'He's a case, darling. Those awful kimonos he wears and the way he puts his tongue out when he thinks he's made a joke. A case and an alcoholic.'

Twice Johann stayed with her in Cambridgeshire, walking about on the balls of his feet, whistling and swearing. He travelled with his typewriter and would set it up in a public part of the house, usually in the hall at a round table. Before spreading himself he would remove the objects which norm- ally occupied it, sending them flying with ferocious impa- tience. Melissa and Polly seethed. They taunted and tormented him. Once he picked up a kitten and sat down to tickle it with nail-bitten fingers. Polly went for him, wrongfully accusing him of ill-treating it.

'Johann. How could you? You're cruel. Put her down. Can't you see you're hurting her?' His dark eyes slipped sideways and he made for the drink tray. Melissa offered him a drink with formality. He exploded.

'Is it wrong to help myself? God, I'm gauche. I'll leave if you want me to. It's not much fun being in a house where you're not wanted.'

Polly, losing patience, mumbled, 'Why come then?' She gathered up the kitten and ran with it up the ancient spooky staircase to her room at the top of the house. Van, desperate for a settlement, began to lose her judgement and her patience.

'When have I ever been intolerant of your friends?' she demanded of Melissa.

'Mum. You know it's different.'

'Why?' she shouted.

Johann winced as Melissa practised the piano. She cocked a sly snook and played with greater force, rattling the keys, making the sound shrill and disagreeable.

A battlefield.

'Christ,' he said to Van. 'Why on earth don't you teach those girls to cook. That, at least, would be useful.'

As she drove him to the station on Monday morning she asked him his plans for the following days; the foul dead days before their next meeting. He replied harshly. 'You must never ask me what I'm doing.'

For the second time since she met him, calamity had struck.

'Why?' she asked, grim with misery. 'You quiz me about my every move.'

'That's different. It would better for you if you didn't. Better for you and better for me.'

She trembled as they kissed goodbye. Pins and needles pierced her fingers. She went to bed for a day and a night, sleeping to shut the horror out. She took long soggy baths, four in a row, without dressing in between. Then he rang, cheery as ever.

He was summoning her to the theatre, and 'I hate to ask you this, but could you pick up a print for me at a gallery in Shepherds Bush on your way? Bless you. Wrap up warm.'

She was up early, picking minute vegetables from the garden. It was spring. She prepared a feast and decanted it into small dishes, covered with silver paper. These she packed into a large hamper, together with two bottles of wine. They were to dine, after the play, at Kennington.

Johann was merry and flirtatious. He looked into her eyes and gripped her elbows with his fingers. It was an awkward position and she wondered if his arms weren't rather long for his body.

'If you should ever lose interest in me I don't know what will become of me. Beautiful woman, and the cleverest I have ever met.'

She said that she never would.

After eating they drew together under the duvet, warm and close. As she fell asleep she thanked him for the happiness and the astonishing peace that invaded her body.

'Fuck!' he said. 'That bloody woman, Melanie, never rang me back. I left two messages on her answering machine and she never even thanked me for lunch on Tuesday. Women are bitches.'

He was soon asleep, snoring and monopolising the duvet.

She tiptoed downstairs and drank herself into a total blank.

The next day he dismissed her, as was his habit, with a kiss and another date.

On the morning of their next outing he brought her a cup of tea in bed. His post had arrived and he was chuckling over the contents of an envelope.

'What do you think of these?' There were six photographs of him, wearing a top hat and tails, spats even. The irresistible leer was spread over his features. 'A girl friend took them at the races last week.'

The roll of fat reappeared and, although she continued to take trouble with her hair and nails, it wasn't working and she knew it.

It was full spring and they talked of Italy and summer plans. They would stay together, he said, either in his house or in hers. Probably hers since, 'Hem, hem,' his was easier to let.

'You drive out with the children,' he proposed. 'I'll follow a little later. Could you take some books out for me? A couple of boxes.' With this long-term plan firmly lodged in her mind, she was at peace.

'When you return home with the children I shall stay on there to write this fucking script and later you will come back to me and we will have some time alone together in the autumn. Perhaps travel a little in France.'

It was settled, and her looks returned. She began to wonder if she was expecting a child. It would not be easy at her age with her girls nearly grown-up and cross. He would tell her what to do. Johann had never had a child and she wanted, with wearisome heartache, to have one, and for him to be the father. It was not as though he would have to marry her. That would be too much to expect. She was well set-up, and there was room in her life and her budget for a bastard. He would be thrilled; overjoyed. Now he would love her fully.

When she knew it to be a fact she spent two days in Cambridge, choosing a dress in which to break the news, dizzy with love. The frilly frock and her new hair cut gave her great confidence and great beauty.

Johann had left a key on a piece of string attached to the inside of his letter-box so that she could let herself in. She found a card scribbled with instructions.

'Have a bath. I won't be long. I've booked a table somewhere nice. I hope you like fish. Take care. Your J.'

She sat still in her new frock. She wasn't nervous any more. Waiting for him she ate an apple and daydreamed. Would she live here if he married her? No. He was only a tenant in the house. Whatever happened she would like to dispose of the duvet. Apart from that she would accept his conditions. Women have to handle difficult men. They are praised for it. It is a virtuous talent. Barriers would fall; gates would open and they would be as one. There would be a stake in his future, and his black eyes would no longer wander. Myra need haunt him no more. (Van had no evidence that Myra occupied his thoughts but, surely, she must.) It was settled.

There was a loud noise in the street. Voices, slamming of doors and the jingling of coins. Johann, drunk as a lord, dismissing his taxi. He came in humming, lurching, talking to himself. He kissed her.

'Hem, hem. Beautiful woman. Have a drink. I'm going to.'

She was happy and amused.

He told her that he had been to visit a friend in hospital. That was why he was a little late. 'Broken bones. Hem. I took her a bottle of champagne.'

She drove to the restaurant where he ordered drinks.

Van put her hand on his arm and told him her news. He sobered up for a second and, once again, his black eyes swivelled, terrified, towards her. She asked him if he was excited.

'Desperately,' he replied. She should have left him there forever but she knew she never could. She would never be able to leave him until he made life impossible for her.

Grinning and drinking all in one, he said 'Carola's here. I've resumed my affair with her.'

'Carola? Johann. You can't. You love me.'

'I shall never tell anyone anything again, it's not worth it. Now you're going to make a fuss. It won't make any difference. No skin off your nose. She asked me if I was going to go on seeing you.'

'What did you say?'

'I said "of course". I told her how much I love you. There. Have another drink.'

She made him pay, and agitated to leave quickly. She fled from the restaurant, head down, her scarf covering her face and hair as though pursued by the press; Johann, unsteady, gripped her fingers in his.

Things would be clear when they got back to the duvet and the noise of the cats with collars. There were objects in the house that she had given him, often at his request. 'Wonderful woman. You who know everything. Where can I get scales? Scales for weighing my mail. Sometimes I send packets and pieces of my script but have no time to go to the post office.' She had found a set, modern and shiny but in the old-fashioned mould with bright, round weights like pieces of gold and a smart glistening stand. They had been expensive but they were perfect and she snapped them up. There was a hearth rug. A nice, cheery hearth rug which she had left in front of his fireplace one day as a surprise. He had never thanked her for it. There were other things in the house, pictures, books and ashtrays that she had provided, and she prayed, in her fear, that once there, the horror would melt.

In the street, weaving towards her car, he ordered her to drive to the club, the one where she had rescued him in his drunken condition the autumn before. His power was frightening. He could not be made pliant. He had to have his drunken head. They sat at high stools alongside the bar. She couldn't have manoeuvred him up the stairs to the parapet where other drinkers sat at tables and where she had found him slumped on the last occasion. They both began a bout of heavy drinking. Van cried and her hands shook.

It was still there, under her new frock. A son. She saw him at the age of forty, tall and strong with a golden moustache, riding a horse or casting for fish. His arms were around her, his elderly mother, drunk and shrivelled and smelling of tobacco. She drank on, knowing that shadows of anility were flickering over her face.

They returned, somehow, to Kennington, hostile and despairing. She asked him what she should do.

'It is entirely up to you. Do as you please. Rub my knuckles. Hard. Hard.'

'Johann, darling. Help me. Carola? Is it true? You can't see us both.'

'Why not, for God's sake?'

'It couldn't work. It won't. I'll go. Don't you see? It can't be the same. What if she's with you when I ring you up?'

'Very often I have a woman with me when you ring me up. Nine times out of ten. I am completely promiscuous you know. Once I had six women in one week.'

She started to retch. Her body was stiff and she cried for the forty-year-old moustached son inside it. His arms were around her and he was telling her that he would love her always in spite of her great age and fragility. He loved her and she would keep him or die with him.

'Van darling,' he called cheerily to her in the morning. 'I can't open my eyes. Fetch a towel. I want you to shave me in bed. Fetch a soft towel and a basinful of warm water. My shaving brush is on the shelf in the bathroom.' He lay there naked, a figure to be wondered at, pectorals sharply defined, buttocks bulging. She must resist.

'Johann. Please. That's not only unreasonable. It's also impossible. I've never shaved anyone in bed in my life.'

'You're being disobliging again.'

His body was compact and muscular. His cock stood out eight inches, circumcised and clean. Was she expected to bandage it? Apply an adhesive wound dressing? Strap it in a splint? Once again she was desperate for a settlement. She suggested shaving him at the basin, a compromise, but he had lost interest and was fiddling with a transistor. It was glued to his ear.

Then he was up, lacing his tea with brandy and listening to sports results. As he shaved he sang and played pat-a-cake with powder in the bathroom. He brought her breakfast in bed. He was wearing a brown velvet dressing-gown which matched his eyes and in which he looked wonderfully handsome. The week before he had complained about his health.

'There's something wrong,' he had said. 'I have asked you this before. Can you make me an appointment with a good doctor? It might be tonsillitis. Have we ever talked of the possibility of my tonsils being responsible?'

She had rung up a Harley Street physician and, as she lay in misery, she remembered that this was the morning for accompanying him to his consultation.

'Hurry,' he said. 'Don't forget you are taking me to your quack. Mustn't be late. I'm terribly excited.'

'What about me, Johann? What do I do? My heart is tormented.'

'When you've dropped me you should think about going to a good one yourself. Do that. Do that and keep me posted.'

# Chapter
## III

An hour later, in the car, near Regent's Park, he turned to her.

'Van. I will support you. I will love you and support you and stand by you for ever. This is my vow.'

Half happy again, she left him on the pavement as near as she could to the wrought-iron door of the main entrance to the doctor's consulting room. Then she did what she knew she must. His vow, although it had brought comfort, had a vacuous ring.

Not one, but three doctors faced her in the psychiatric department. It was Van's first introduction to that profession and, really, there was no need. Her mind was unnaturally clear; her emotions strong and true.

A tall young woman asked 'Why don't you want the child, dear?' As she spoke she looked at the form Van had filled in at a desk on the floor below.

'Is it your age, dear?' Then she looked, again, at the paper and saw that she was dealing with a widow. 'Or your circumstances?'

Another doctor, a man with a baby face and tufts of hair growing out of his nose, said, 'I'd better examine her if it's a question of age. Hop up on here.' He pointed to a couch behind a curtain. Van looked from one to the other, ignoring the third, a shrivelled fellow barely more than a lad. She said softly, 'Really I don't know.'

The tall woman tried again. 'Well. You're here, dear, so, presumably, you're asking for termination. You'd better do the talking. What's the father like?'

Van exploded.

'He doesn't expect my forgiveness. I can't shame him. I mean he's ashamed to his full capacity. He behaves as if, just by admitting he's impossible, he has emerged sanctified. I can't move him and yet I can't stop trying.'

All three looked in pity at the woman sitting amongst them, lost in her own thicket of despair. She was given tea and blood tests, and her body was hurt and humbled. There were no problems when it came to the signing of the termination papers. She paid and departed, permission granted for further torments.

On the way to the clinic, in outer London, Van found her map hard to follow. She asked the way of a taxi driver, giving only the street name of her destination. The face of a toad leered at her through the taxi window but she had no wish to kiss its lips.

'On your way to the clinic, dear?' The street was, clearly, notorious. Van glared; dignified.

'I have no time whatsoever in which to share a joke,' she told him.

Taking pity, the toad guided her, taking his time, to a turreted house in the suburbs. Van remembered something about a midwife toad but she couldn't think what it was. Beside the door bell there was a plaque. Three words were written on it, one on top of the other; Jour. Tag. Giorno. She fingered the word Tag. Johann's paternal tongue. The room inside was full of girls, foetuses squirming about in their innards. Some sat alone and some beside boy friends. Van wondered if any of them were near to her in age. A howling waif sat at her side. Plants in pots were nearly dead; no time here, with this volume of traffic, for cosseting clutter.

Soon Johann would bounce in. He would be at her side; pinch her cheek and take her away. He might have had the duvet cover cleaned and puffed up pillows. There was no way of his knowing where she was. She recollected, vaguely, something about his having booked in at a health farm; a new one with startling equipment. Still, somehow or other, he would come. There was a sign pinned to the wall. 'If you're happy with your pregnancy FINE. If not PHONE.' Beside and under this there were a great many advertisements for con-traceptives. Even a calendar carried the theme. The girls in charge were downright sloppy. Huge fat cows ambling about with lists in one hand; with the other hand they drank coffee from white plastic cups that changed shape as they gave way beneath podgy fingers. Two untidy girls giggled and smoked; probably regulars. They seemed to know the ropes.

More than anything Van dreaded the blood test. What a waste. Johann would have revelled in it. Her face was covered in spots. She noticed them as she passed a mirror. They must have erupted, just like that, on her way to the clinic. If only he would walk in now, the day would be saved. She searched her mind for clues. Had she let some small word drop that might lead him to her?

Girls were herded in clusters of three. Van was bracketed with Deborah, alone and crying bitterly, and with Tracy, older even than Van and cared for, gently, by a man.

They were led away into a tiny room where a slimy cyclamen with yellow stalks drooped over an advertisement for Maximits – disposable examination gloves. She glared at specimen bottles. These had tags around their necks saying 'for re-cycle only'. Then there was something called a Vacutainer which boasted a new method of taking blood, shuvstrips (skin closures) and, for some reason, sterile eye-drops. Johann would have gone berserk among such goodies.

A big Jamaican nurse handed them two valiums each and water in mugs from the plastic store. It would be too late now, even if he arrived at the clinic. How would he find her in this cubicle with the slimy cyclamen? The pills settled her and she didn't care any more. Johann could, at least, have provided her with these. She hoped the same thing would happen to Carola one day. Why should she get off scot free? At one o'clock she came round from the anaesthetic and saw Deborah weeping in the next bed. Tracy was cheerful and asked if her husband could come in.

Van assured the nurse that somebody was calling for her; that he was waiting round the corner in a car. She wobbled out.

When she looked in the driving mirror she saw that her face was yellow. Yellow and plastered, still, with huge red spots. It was a day of unprecedented rain. At pressure from her foot the car went forward and she seemed, at last, to be in charge of something. The car was behaving exactly as she would have wished although the weather was unkind. She drew it out, too fast, from the kerb and caused a taxi to swerve. The driver shot his head through the open window, leaning across to reach it past his meter. He was an albino and his spectacle lenses were spotless.

'Are you a damned, fucking, sodding, bloody bastard?' he demanded.

Van stared, very polite.

'No,' she said. 'I'm not. I'm afraid it must be a case of mistaken identity.'

Johann might be waiting for her at home. He knew, if he had taken in any single detail of her life, that Melissa and Polly were both away at school. All would be well. She would have her baby after all. Johann would be proud of her and her spots would fall off.

The house was empty. Van let herself in with a key that she had attached to a piece of string and hung around her neck. It took three quarters of an hour to cross the hall, climb the stairs and fall across her bed. In the night she felt her limbs shake till the bed quivered under her. Every nerve in her body, strung up to the uttermost point of fear, at last gave way. Her brain was paralysed. She sat, shuddering, by the foot of her bed to watch out the hours till morning.

Johann rang her from a health farm and asked her if she was ready for a joke. He had been massaged that morning, he told her, by a Japanese beauty and, by coincidence, she had plastered him in a cream called Carola.

Also he was thinking of giving a party. In fact he had already made out a preliminary list of guests but couldn't decide whether the Kennington house was large enough for such entertainment. He was anxious that she should help him and invite a few of her friends along to liven things up.

'Johann. You're mad,' she said. 'What are you celebrating? Which of us do you invite? I'm ill. I'm in bed.'

'Come on. You're over-reacting about this Carola business. It won't last a week. I'll send her packing. I'm not losing you. Let's give a party.'

'I can't walk.'

'You'll be able to by then. You're brave. You've often told me how brave you are.'

He didn't ask about her health or her ordeal. He never mentioned it. Too pleased with his joke and his party plans.

He wrote:

Darling.

It's over with Carola. I'm sorry if I hurt you. You are a very emotional woman. The most emotional woman I have ever met. Sometimes I fear for you. Please may I stay with you next weekend? There's a party in your neighbourhood. Will you come with me as my partner? I'm allowed to bring a girl friend. Take care. Big X.

Johann.

She wasn't well but she was determined to accompany him to the party. She crawled around preparing meals and tidying the house. She wanted him to be comfortable even though there turned out to be very little the matter with him. His tonsils were quite in order. The doctor had suggested an allergy to coffee. Perhaps Johann had held back vital information concerning other habits.

Carola had gone. So had Van's forty-year-old son.

She met him at the station on Friday afternoon. He was in full morning dress as she had seen him in the photograph taken at the races. He carried a top hat and lavender gloves. Round coloured labels were pinned on his lapels. He was mildly drunk and smoking a cigarette. Once home he asked her if she would run his bath. Van had never seen the point of one human being running the bath of another; the timing was complicated and there was always the possibility of misunderstanding and overflows. She refused, and he told her she was the most disobliging woman he had ever met. Later she wished that she had been obedient, for he allowed it to splash over and water appeared below, leaving a stain on the kitchen ceiling.

That night she wore a dress of startling glamour. Polly was vexed that this sublime creation should be taken from its wrapping and worn for a carousal with Kraesel. From time to time she had fingered it and asked her mother when it would be worn.

'Oh. I don't know, duck. I never do anything glamorous any more. Let's just have a squizz at it now and then.' The mysterious frock was now on the loose – wrapped around Vanessa for an evening with the kraut. Everything was awful and her mother wasn't well. Polly knew this from the look in her eyes and the strained notes of her voice. Weekends out from school had been rapturous in the past.

Johann was pleased with her.

'Beautiful woman. We will stop for a drink.'

'Like this? Johann, we can't. I can't go into a pub like this.'

'Why are you so disobliging today?'

Her legs were wobbly and barely capable of holding her weight. Heavily made up and strapped into the expensive frock she looked fine. He was attentive to her at the party, pleased with her looks and her ability to amuse people around her. He danced vigorously, looking a little odd with his hooked nose and general unsteadiness. At one point he deserted her. Later she discovered that he had been kissing the hostess down by the swimming pool.

There were people and flowers and a merry band in a tent which was full of round tables surrounded by fragile gold chairs. As the party emptied out, Van noticed him sitting, more or less normally, on one of these chairs. It was rootless, pulled away from its table and sticking out into a passageway which led from the tent to the garden. It was a moment before she realised that he was unconscious and that fellow-guests were giving him a wide berth. His eyes remained open, inert black marbles. An oozing outflow of saliva left his lips and ran down his chin onto the bow tie she had knotted for him after his disorganised bath.

A woman, a blonde, went to him and cradled his head in her arms. She drew a chair up alongside his and allowed the top half of his lifeless body to fall, slowly, onto her lap. She was a foxy little thing. Her black frock, fastened around her tiny waist by a silver chain, was low cut. Fair hair, reaching her shoulders, was set like enamel. Van feared that her nails would break were she to tap it.

Lady into Fox. Van wondered if a bushy tail was forming between those tightly encased buttocks. A memory came to her of the fox she had nearly run over when visiting Carola's aunt on her way to make enquiries about Johann. Faced with this human fox her heart didn't turn over, but hardened instead. Wiping the stream of saliva from his mouth with a paper table-napkin, the vixen let her stiff hair brush Johann's face. Van joined them and disengaged the drunken arms.

Her legs and arms felt brittle and crumbly as she kicked off her dancing shoes. Unaided she pulled Johann from the tent and across a dewy field, dawn breaking, to her car. As she drove home his heaviness increased and his immobility frightened her as did the saliva flow, which continued its relentless course.

By morning she had put him to bed, first removing his clothes and then sponging his face. She bathed and changed, and, without lying down, met the day and the daughters who had friends of their own staying in the house.

'How was the party, Mum?'

'Fine, but poor Johann may be rather the worse for wear.'


He did not appear until late afternoon. Unabashed, he asked if he could borrow a wireless, a belt and a nail file. Also he wanted to make some telephone calls. He helped himself to a drink and asked if he could borrow the car. He had been invited to another party in the neighbourhood. No suggestion of taking her with him this time. He wouldn't have another drink that day, he said. That was a promise.

Wrenching her car, her most treasured possession, into reverse gear, he cursed her from the driver's seat for its shortcomings.

'Time you got a decent car. In this you are a danger to others.' No mention of herself.

In a series of fits and startled leaps, he rattled off.

That night he did not return.

Van woke, her tummy aching and her heart in tatters, at around six o'clock. She looked into the room allotted to Johann and saw only the unmade bed, jumbled from his day in it. She had planned to tidy and prepare it for his return but her strength had failed. The top hat was on a chair by the dressing-table. The morning passed. The girls said nothing. Van was thankful for that. A conspiracy of gentle silence calmed the house. Perhaps her daughters pitied her for the mire she floundered in.

Johann returned as they were sitting down to lunch. He asked her to go out into the hall with him.

His face was white and waxy, his whole appearance one of soggy squelchiness. There was a stratum of sweat over his being and it seemed he was going to faint.

'Van,' he said. 'Beautiful Van. I'm in a bad way. I didn't want to pass out again last night so I took pills. Pills, and plenty of whisky.'

'As long as you didn't drink coffee,' she said. 'Remember your allergy.'

'Very funny. Hem, hem. Very funny. For that I shall go to bed.'

This was an idle boast. He fell, heavy as lead, to the ground. Melissa and her friends, with ill-hidden delight, carted him up to the unmade bed where they dumped his body, careful to place the top hat over his dribbling face. Polly had skipped lunch and was walking, by herself, in a boggy nature reserve beyond the church, outside the village boundary.

Melissa found her mother in the kitchen. Van was clearing plates, stacking them into a machine beside the sink.

'I don't think we'll see much more of Johann today, Mum.'

'Poor fellow. He's not well. Give us a hand.' Grimly she brushed Melissa's overtures aside. If she craved Johann's presence then her girls must put up with it. It was a bloody fight. It wasn't easy to protect a man who did nothing to help her in his cause.

Her condition was serious. She had no power, no authority, over Johann. She supposed that this was the exemplification of love.

She avoided her uncle. He would have insisted on protecting her. She was too far gone.

Several times after her experience at the clinic, she had yearned to confide in him. Often she had ached to dial his number but resisted. He would have abominated Johann's behaviour and been outraged that she could still contemplate allowing him to come to the house – inflicting his presence on the guileless and affectionate girls who had, hitherto, looked to her for love and counsel.

She was being mangled and there was no escape.

Carola had exerted some evil influence over him, she was sure.

Van envisaged them conspiring together; heads close, bodies intertwined. A Charles Adams pair, she saw them as, lean and sinewy, sniggering over the invention of possible torments. That night they bore down on her as she lay beside the fire on a hearth-rug that Uncle Jim had stitched for her during his evenings with Gordon. The gros-point pattern was colourful and flowery. It helped her dream herself to sleep. The visiting pair entered the room silently, pointed to her and cackled in united mirth.

Van wondered, the next morning, whether Carola really had departed or whether she had received one of the many telephone calls Johann had made two days before. Perhaps she had been at the party he had driven to, alone, in her car.

Johann was jaunty when he awoke, and ready to return to Kennington. She tackled him about Carola.

'It's over,' he said, 'and that's all there is to it. Let it go now for Christ's sake. Can I help myself to vegetables, spinach or whatever is on the go?' He strutted down to the vegetable garden.

When she helped him take his things out of the car at the station, she glanced into the plastic bag, now bulging, which he had carried with him to the garden. There was, indeed, some spinach, also a few potatoes, onions and carrots from her precious winter store in the potting-shed. Well, he had asked for vegetables and she had agreed but what struck her as odd was the sight of a large bunch of primroses plucked, presumably, from a bank by the stream. Funny to help yourself to flowers without mentioning it.

Soon it was summer and she laid her plans. These plans involving Johann, were as much as she could handle. Other tasks held no relevance. Her mind was set in this single track. She looked, despairingly, at her garden.

Here was another jungle of her own making.

She had created it but could not, now, tend it. Spinach bolted and strawberries ripened, mushy and unpicked. The deep-freeze sat inactive, open and empty, switched off at source and warm within. Lettuces, jammed tight in rows, threatened each other as the broad beans grew and swelled. Carrots, tender and new, perfect for drawing, lost their freshness. Potatoes, round and waxy, bulged in the earth. Years before, Van had seen a play with Martin that had made them laugh. A lady, a neighbour, had been paid to come each day to eat left-over food. Should she pay the vicar's wife to pick and freeze and eat the spoils of her garden? Soon the plums would ripen, then raspberries, miracles from celibate twigs she had jammed into a narrow bed beside the wall. Radishes rotted and rose plants, heavy with dead petals, damp and mouldy, hung their heads in mortification. Gooseberries were ripe, mature; ready with a sprinkling of elderflower, to be reordered into sorbets. Beetroots, tender when young, were hardening; forming dark skins and hollow shredded innards, like her own.

Goose-grass sprouted from border clumps erratic as her

state of mind. Blackened cones, drop-earrings, lay stinking against pale lilac leaves and apples, hard and green, lowered boughs by several inches.

She would leave for Tuscany, by car, loaded with Johann's books, at the end of July. Johann would join her in mid-August. They would be there together with the children and other guests for two weeks and then she would have to leave him alone to write his interminable film-script. She had to be in England in early September for the wedding of a niece. She was very tired and the thought of these high-pressure journeys daunted her and almost made her lose her nerve. However, she was spurred on by the involvement of Johann in her plans.

After the wedding and after settling the girls she would return to him, again by car, and be with him for several weeks.

Together they would drive back to England.

'I will treat you to a gastronomic tour,' he promised.

'Yum. Yum.' He patted his belly. That way his books would be returned; he had planned another year in Kennington. England suited him and the owner of the house seemed happy to continue with the arrangement.

His party did not take place or, if it did, she heard no more about it.

Two nights before she left he took her to a concert at the Barbican. As on other occasions he had left the key on a piece of string inside his letter-box with a note attached to it.

'Darling. This will be our first outing. Go to the bedroom and you will find a flower on the bed. Pin this onto your dress. Meet me at the Barbican and don't be shocked by the building. It's hideous but the concert will be good. Love you madly. Johann.'

There, on the bed, was a prickly red rose beside a bottle of scent, an unfamiliar type in an octagonal bottle. It smelled sickly and she emptied half the contents onto her arms and frock.

Never had he been so loving or looked so dashing. He kissed her curls and pulled her close to him. In the interval they sat on an open terrace. He ordered white wine to be brought to them and they drank, talking of her departure.

'Soon we will be together. Two short partings and then our

holiday. This is our first outing. We begin from the beginning. I love you madly and I shall miss you.'

It had come out right.

On the stairs that night he made a vow to her. It was the same as the one he had made before in Regent's Park on the way to his appointment with the doctor.

'Van darling. I will love you. I will stand by you and support you for ever. That is my vow.' She wondered if he remembered having said this before and thought of her moustached son riding bareback. In the morning, very early, he demonstrated his love without, as far as she knew, the help of green pills.

'Now,' he said, ogling his eyes, 'please my darling. Take me to Bethnal Green. My typewriter is playing me up and I'm lost without it. Utterly lost.'

She was crestfallen. There was so much to do before leaving England the following day. Every moment was mapped out. He looked angry and she relented.

'Good girl,' he said. 'Good and beautiful.'

He wrote to her from London.

You are lucky to be in Italy. It is hell here. I spend my time working. There are few people about and those who are are getting on each others' nerves. I miss you dreadfully. I haven't left London and I won't until I join you. Longing to see you. Can you meet me at Pisa station? I have decided to come by train. Ring me but not too early. I am working late and will want to sleep in. Big X.

Van was happy to be back in her house but nervous of going to the town for fear of meeting Carola and of knowing so little about her brief reunion with Johann earlier in the year. Her thoughts dwelt retrospectively on that episode and she retched into the wash-basin. She had been planning to wash her hair. She was sicking up her son. Carola had gagged and bound Johann, forbidden him to show her mercy or to share his misery.

Van seldom went further than the village and busied herself preparing treats for his arrival. Two giant pots of basil were installed outside the kitchen door. Omelette pans and kitchen utensils were ordered so that he could enjoy cooking, particularly during his time alone there.

Melissa and Polly were out more often, even, than before.

Van was solitary, but decided to make an exception of James and Henry. They were her firmest friends and farmed nearby, working to a schedule, a taut timetable, and needed warning before interruptions. They tilled and toiled, pruned and gleaned, from dawn to dusk. There would be no bumping into Carola there. Some years before their house had been described in a novel by a handsome American writer, David Plante, in the form of a letter.

James and Henry had given Van a copy of the book and the memory of the description, of the accuracy of the author, made her smile as she drove along the rough road one day to visit them.

He had called them Charles, a composite figure.

It is beautiful here. Charles's villa is eighteenth century, built by local builders who obviously knew nothing about architectural plans; the corners are not exact, the symmetry is off, the stone is heavy, the plaster rather thick, as on a peasant's house. And yet all of it fits into and fills out one very large impression; mottled pink walls, shuttered windows, a double staircase, pine trees, palm trees, and a walled garden of thick flowers, vines, flowering trees, huge wet terracotta pots of fruit trees. In one corner of the garden, beyond Charles's great pride, a lotus pool, is a chapel, still consecrated, a small dark crumbling stone box with a very few dusty vestiges of its sanctity; rather gray and wet altar cloths, broken candle sticks, a crucifix with broken arms, a holy-water font stuck in the wall and lighter areas on the walls where pictures had been: there are even two pews, a cobwebbed wine bottle occupying one; the stations of the cross – small framed colored pictures – are still in place. Today I saw a peasant woman (one of a warped strange family who live in the farm cottages just outside the villa's gates) cutting roses by the chapel to put inside, before a shrine. I go into the chapel often; it's my favourite building – that, and the wine cellar of the cantina, a long dark beamed hall filled with enormous tuns, demijohns, great green bottles, and very worn out wooden contraptions for preparing the grapes. Charles has his own wine, olive oil, fruit, vegetables, cheese, eggs, poultry, nuts, berries. The land, planted partly for hay, partly for vines, partly olive grove, slopes down to a small stream and pond in a dense cool very green wood. The valley is terraced with vines, and here and there are cottages and blue black cypresses. Poppies are still out, and yellow daisies, and lots and lots of tiny lavender flowers. Charles has filled the villa itself with what he has been collecting for years; bronzes, huge leather bound books, heavy medallions placed on small round tables, rugs, furniture. All the floors are red tile, the walls are white-washed.

Van sat with James and Henry beside the lotus pool amongst the flowering trees and looked down to the chapel. How different it was from Kennington and the life in London bars that she led with Johann.

One of her schemes was to provide her lover with company during the gap in her visits. Who knew but that Carola might commence pursuit the minute Van's back was turned? There would be no transport for him and no telephone. His own rusty Fiat was let, along with his house, part of a package deal. In spite of being familiar with the district, as he had made clear to her during their first telephone conversation, it seemed that he had few friends and was ostracised by the neighbours. Van wondered if it had anything to do with Myra's death and whether people resented his inheritance of her property. Indeed, and it came to her with a shock, she had never heard of him before he called her from Hamburg and, although he was seldom there, they had, presumably, been part-time neighbours for several years.

Searching for distractions, she tested her imaginative powers. Not only must Johann be distracted but also Polly and Melissa. They would have to be amused and prevented, at all costs, from continuing their private battle with Johann. Each time either of her girls had suggested inviting a friend to stay, Van had nodded dumbly.

She no longer dared to limit or restrict them and the house

was filling up, putting extra strain on domestic arrangements.

The best bedroom, the one that was usually reserved for Uncle Jim, was held, clean and sacred, for Johann.

Van hadn't pressed her uncle to join them that year. It was the first time he had ever skipped a summer visit.

A letter came from him one afternoon. Rosina, a stout lady, spiralled up the drive with it on an orange vespa. She wore a grey post-office uniform. Normally Van collected her post from the man who sold gas bombolas and who lived in a strategic village spot, convenient for passers-by. This saved the tyres of Rosina's bike from the ruts in the drive. On this occasion she came in person. There was talk down below of strange goings on at the villa and Rosina was curious to count the heads up there. It was a fruitless trip, but she liked to exclaim on the startling changes Melissa and Polly had undergone in the months that had passed.

Van opened Uncle Jim's letter in her room, before tossing it into the wooden cupboard beside her bed. She had hoped for another one from Johann.

Darling.

I hate not to be with you this year. I had a feeling that you were full up what with the girls all bringing friends. Let's go alone together when they're back at school. I hope you didn't expect me to propose myself? There's never been any need for formal invitations between us has there? Perhaps I've been over-sensitive. I only hope I haven't let you down in any way.

How could she have had Uncle Jim to stay with Johann calling him a Bertie Woofter and cooking all over the house? It was yet another muddle of her own making.

Rupert and Lucy, many years younger than she, lived further south in the Chianti country. They were always cheerful and ready for almost anything. They had a new convertible car and liked to cruise around in it. They, she knew, would support her in any scheme and would be amused by Johann and prepared, temporarily at least, to fit in with his drinking habits.

She booked them to stay with her for the second half of August so they could meet Johann before she left for England.

Melissa asked, 'Why's the spare-room all tidged up? Is it for Rupert and Lucy?' Van had been elusive about plans.

'No duck. Johann's coming. He's renting the house for a bit after we go and I'll need to have him here before we leave to show him how things work. His own is let and I needed some money.' She was lying again; making out there was a business transaction.

Melissa and Polly grumbled together beside the pool.

Looking brown and well, she was at Pisa station before the appointed hour of Johann's arrival.

A curmudgeonly face met hers. His hands were full of a dripping, greasy packet and his clothes were in disarray.

'I didn't get a wink on that fucking train. Here's some terrine for you from Paris. I stopped off there for a night to see some friends. God. What a journey.'

If he had stopped in Paris, he could not have been in much of a rush to see her. He asked if his books were safe and what the plans were for his stay. Withering inside, voice uncontrolled, she outlined the days ahead, telling him of Rupert's and Lucy's visit and other trips she had arranged. He perked up and, once through the tunnel which pierced the Pisan hills, he pinched her cheek.

The terrine worried him. It was exposed to the sun in the back there with his luggage. They must have it for lunch today. Van knew that Melissa and Polly would hate it, never to be budged from pasta and salami. She would have to stuff it all into herself and make appreciative noises. This was only the beginning. In the days to follow there were no signs of his vow. He banged away at his typewriter, issuing expletives, making demands.

Swimming in shiny black briefs, his head would go down under the water where he would keep it for anything up to a minute, then, raising it, he would let a long spurt of water shoot upwards into the air. This would be followed by a few heavy breaths, and then it would be repeated.

'Johann. What are you doing?' Melissa asked.

'Exhaling.'

Clasping his head with both hands, clamping them hard, he lamented.

'Christ, I'm buzzing in both ears. There must be something the matter with the pool. It's contaminated.'

Bilharzia in her swimming-pool.

She had gone to so much trouble, commissioning major repairs on the filter machine. The water was clear and blue, her pride and joy.

'Christ Almighty woman! It must be infected. I'll have to have them syringed. Have you got a syringe?'

She was frail, impotent.

'Listen to this,' he said, coming close, nipples outstanding, briefs bulging. 'I'm wheezing. God alive. I'm a dying man. Have you got a stethoscope in the house? Listen to my chest.'

Perhaps she could buy one, that and a syringe, in the orthopaedic shop. His kinks were catching.

Van's daughters turned him into a figure of fun.

He was cooking, once again, in a yellow kimono. Melissa peered into the kitchen.

'Good luck with the bubble and squeak. Don't exhale into it.'

There followed mocking laughter around the house.

There was a golden moment when Rupert and Lucy arrived. Everybody responded to their high spirits.

Johann forgot to type and spent hours with Rupert concocting a stupefying drink, filling the inside of a water-melon with a mixture of rum and vodka pulped together with the juice of the fruit and a handful of ice-cubes. He tiptoed around handing out glasses of the shocking pink liquid. The three would go to Lucca together and return with loads of newspapers and reinforcements for the drink cupboard. Van was always in terror that he would meet Carola and fail to reappear. One night when, under the influence of Rupert and of wine, he was making a fuss of her for the first time since his arrival, she asked him about Carola.

'Don't spoil it. She's in America.'

'How do you know – and spoil what?'

'Come on darling. We're having a lovely time. I love your friends. In fact they've asked me to go and stay with them for a wine festival when you're back in England. They're coming here for a few days for the Lucca opera. Sad that you'll miss it. There, my sweet. I love you madly. No more questions.'

Rupert and Lucy had to move on but promised to return as soon as Van left. They were loyal watchdogs.

'Then we'll see lots of you when you get back,' Rupert promised.

Things slipped after their departure and Johann was cross again, avoiding chances of being alone with her. They couldn't share a bed with so many young ones in the house.

It was her last day. The teenagers left the house early for a farewell visit to the sea.

Then they were by themselves. Johann was lying on the lawn in his black briefs, his face greasy with sun-lotion, trying to read his newspaper without it shading him and spoiling his chances of getting a tan.

She sat beside him and asked him point blank if he remembered the vows he had made her.

'God. You are a one for raking up the past,' he said. 'Please darling. Let me finish this article. It's interesting. I know you never read the papers. There.' He pinched her arm and gave her a half-hearted leer.

'What would you like to do today?' Now she was relentless. Desperate.

'Oh, lie in the sun. Work a bit. That sort of thing. I've got some hard drinking to do in the days to come with Rupie and Lucy.' Nobody had ever called him Rupie.

'But Johann. It's my last day. Darling. Please.'

'So it is. O.K. Shall we do some sight-seeing? I don't particularly want to but – well – anything you say.'

'Shall we take a picnic to the hills?'

'If you say so.'

This was her forte. She could prepare a picnic hamper with

imagination and skill. He would love it. Gathering up cushions, carafes and a basket of figs, she willed it to do the trick. To make him happy with her as he had been the night he took her to the Barbican before she left England.

On an olive terrace, up in the hills, beside a crumbling farm house, they spread out rugs, crushing thyme and other four-letter words with their feet and belongings.

Suddenly the sky was overcast and the rain began to drop upon them. It happened in an instant or perhaps she had not noticed the weather in her agony of mind. She hoped that they would huddle together in the ruined building until the rain stopped but Johann said:

'No. No point. It's here to stay. Sorry about your picnic but it's home for me. Home and a sleep.'

Frantic, she slid, uninvited, into bed beside him. He gave her an arm to rub but she had no strength.

'Tomorrow,' she said, 'I must go home. I leave you in my house, enjoying the company of my friends, living my life. I drive a thousand miles, turn around and do the same in order to be with you. I've been ill and bereft. Now I want to know. Why do you avoid me? What is the position with Carola?'

'Oh Van. Don't spoil it. I don't know. There. That's the truth if you want it. I don't know.'

'Have you been seeing her in London this summer when you said it was all over? Were you with her after I came out here?'

'If you say so.'

Worst fears confirmed. That is the cruellest thing.

'How have you left it? Are you in love with her?'

'I don't know.'

'Why did you come here?'

'Because I love you too. I didn't want to lose you. Haven't you ever heard of a man being in love with two women at once?'

'Yes. And I know it to be impossible.'

'You are impossible.'

There was a noise below. Melissa and Polly with their group of friends were returning from the sea, driven back by the bad weather. She was in her own room before they entered the house, lying at one moment in disbelief and at another in torment. She wrote a note and pushed it under Johann's door. He would not see it for a while since she could hear his snores through the ill-fitting frame. The note was not a cry for help. That, she knew, would have gone unanswered. She was demanding further torture – that of the truth. Supposing he had had a conscious thought as she was dragging his lifeless body across the field at dawn after his performance at the party, would it have been of Carola? She must know. The worst had happened already. There was little more to fear. In the brief note she demanded that he should tell her everything or leave, before she did, the following morning.

He appeared, refreshed by his sleep, offering to take her to dinner in Lucca.

'Before dining,' he said 'could you take me to the bus station? I shall need a timetable when I'm stranded alone up here. That's to say before Rupie gets back.'

His face was buried in the timetable as he came out of the bus station.

'Wonderful,' he said. 'They go every hour, straight past the bottom of your drive. I bet you never knew that. Fresh pasta! You told me there was a good shop near here. I'd like to stock up before you go. One can't do much shopping on public transport.'

There was no question of her going into the shop with him. It would have made her ill to hear him ordering shapes and sizes in a variety of colours. Instead she walked ahead and hid herself on the steps of an ancient building. A gloomy old palazzo. He did not notice her there as he walked, very fast, past her feet. It was tempting to allow him to disappear and cause confusion. He would only return to the car and make her look paltry, so she caught up with him and he held her arm in an iron grip.

At the Bar delle Mura, where he had limped away with Uncle Jim's newspapers almost exactly a year before, she pressed her point.

'Have you been away with her for a weekend? I mean this summer?'

Trapped and huffy, he said, 'Yes. Once.'

'What did you tell me you were doing? We were in constant touch.'

'You were here. It was after you left. We went to Northumberland to stay with some friends of hers. A bearded squire and his lady friend.'

She had left on a Saturday. So, after being driven by her with his typewriter to Bethnal Green, after their night together and their new dawn, (rose pinned to her frock, drenched in cheap scent), after their tender farewell, he had travelled to Northumberland the same night with Carola. He had written to her saying that he was bored and lonely; that he had not left London.

Tears rolled down her cheeks and she took his hand, unbelieving.

'I'm terribly unwell. Unwell and unhappy.'

'I know, my sweet. Don't be. There's no need.'

'Are you going to see her again?'

'I daresay. I have to go to London for a few days on business. Before you return here. I may see her then. She lives in London now.'

London! He had made plans of which she knew nothing. At some moment unknown to her, behind her back, he had altered the pattern; arranged a quick flip to London. Blackness hit her brain. Again her worst fears were hazily confirmed. Within him there was a life separate from hers. It was agonising. Calls had been made. Communications, intimacies had taken place. He was planning to see Carola. Van had not been consulted. He was here, surely, because they loved each other. It was impenetrable. Rage welled, smashing the good in her. She would make it impossible, out of the question. Somehow she would cover him, hem him in. Determination took over; determination to spare herself the final insult; to save him, even, from inflicting it. If he couldn't destroy her, despite his intent, all would be well. It would blow over, wouldn't have occurred.

But should she fight? Would each victory be a Pyrrhic one? Her flesh was mortified. Every inch of it. He knew it all; had tried it out; put it to every test. That had held her safe but it hadn't satisfied him. Perhaps anybody would have done. Any old body. Was her sense of her own identity too strong? Maybe she was conceited, maybe unrobust.

'Why does she live in London? Because of you?'

'Who knows? She says she is in love with me.'

'What about me?'

'I shall see you both.'

'One each night?'

'That's enough. Let's go and dine.'

There was cruelty in his face. He had come because he wanted a quiet spot, rent-free, in which to finish his script. She loved him more than ever.

'Doesn't Carola wonder why you came?'

'Yes. She does. She's furious. It may have put an end to our affair. So there. I have made a sacrifice in order to be with you. Isn't that enough?'

She could not leave it alone. It was a scab. She should have left it to drop off of its own accord one day, but her strength was not equal to this. The interminable drive before her, up the autostrada past Genoa and through the Alps, was somewhere in her mind, a menace behind the misery. Later, when they were at home, he promised her that it would be over with Carola. He would write to her the following day. He would explain. Van would return and they would have their gastronomic tour through France as planned. She would meet him at London airport, that was her suggestion, and they would spend those few days together when he returned on business. Carola meant nothing to him. It had been a mistake. She had swamped him and he had been out of his depth. He had lied in order not to lose her. He was sorry and he loved her.

She awoke no longer dreading the drive, thinking only of his few days in London and of her return to Italy. Her plans were full of him. Nothing had altered. They would talk of her son and he would understand what she had suffered.

Off they sped, Johann in his kimono waving to them from the terrace. Van had cut it fine and the wedding was upon them.

That night they all, Van, Melissa and Polly, squeezed into one room of a boarding house near Toulon. The beds were hard. Long bumpy bolsters served as pillows. A basin and a bidet were concealed behind a flapping plastic curtain. The walls were no more than flimsy partitions and, as Van willed herself to sleep, she heard noises from the room next door, noises so raucous that they became a part of her. Melissa and Polly slept. A pair in the adjoining room expressed their passion for each other with boisterous verve throughout the night. Occasionally there would be a lull when, presumably, her neighbours banked some sleep. Van smiled and rested.

The niece's wedding took-place in a Cornish village. Drivers had been warned about the difficulty of crawling up the narrow main street and dressy guests walked the last bit, some clasping hats to their heads in the wind. There were people from the past, and Van stood outside the church for as long as she dared before the bride appeared on the arm of her father. Quite suddenly a wasp stung her on the fleshy underside of her thumb and it began to swell and to irritate. She hit out, partly in order to dislodge the wasp and partly from surprise. Her hand struck an elderly woman in the stomach, making her bend over and cry. Van attempted to explain, exhibiting her swelling finger. Then she had to take her place in a pew. Uncle Jim was there already and had kept her a seat beside him. He whispered that he was longing for a chat. The service began and tears ran down her cheeks. Some of these tears were caused by the pain in her thumb and some by the memory of her last day with Johann in Tuscany: of the picnic in the rain by the deserted farm buildings. As her niece made vows at the altar she thought of the vows Johann had made to her, and wondered if he would have cherished them had they been made in a church. At the party, following the service, Van's brother, father of the bride, introduced her to an Australian girl called Cheryl.

Van recognised the name. Johann had, at some stage, spoken of her. Tall and dressed in black, Cheryl came very close, eyes animated.

'Don't you know Johann Kraesel? He's asked me to visit him at some villa he's rented in Tuscany. He's let his own. I gather he's taken up with his old flame, Carola. She took over from me. I said I wouldn't go if she was there. There's a photo of them in one of the weeklies at some party or other. Did you see it?'

She could see nothing. The gleaming eyes of her interlocutor were as behind a veil. It would never end. The wheel of torture was carrying her up and round and down. How could he have allowed himself to be photographed with Carola at a party knowing that it might appear in a magazine? He hadn't cared enough to hide his tracks.

Uncle Jim was hemmed in by ageing relations and Van gave him the slip. It would be impossible to react to the sound advice he would, unquestionably, give her and she didn't want to let him down.

It was raining on the day she was to meet Johann at the airport. She had got wet and cold while filling a basket and a box or two with provisions from the garden – more than enough to last out Johann's three-day visit.

He charged through the barrier wearing a red rugger shirt, jeans and a canvas jacket. He carried a sort of satchel. The bulk of his wardrobe was left behind in Tuscany. Embracing her, he planted a dry kiss on her lips.

Back in Kennington she was neglected whilst he checked on his mail, his possessions and answering machine messages.

The buzzing in his ears, contracted from some foreign body in her swimming-pool, still bothered him. Attention was called for.

A form, requested by post from Italy, had been sent to him by authorities at the hospital near Kennington. They asked for details, needing to know the nature of the complaint before arranging the length of and department for the consultation. Would the patient be requiring the services of an ambulance? He placed a tick in the square available. A stretcher? Another tick.

'By the way,' he told her later, 'I'm sueing that fucking hospital. I ticked for an ambulance and a stretcher and what do I get? A summons to the outpatients in a month's time. I may not even be here.'

She had hemmed him in, she knew, and he could not slip away. She was sealing his visit by her presence, leaving him no scope.

As they drank wine, settled by the brightly coloured hearth-rug, he asked her how long she intended to stay. Nobody was going to get the better of him.

'I shall stay until you leave, Johann.'

'I may be here for a week. You can't stay as long as that. What about your children? Surely you have to visit them? Three days was what we decided.'

'I shall stay until you leave.'

'You can't. You simply can't.'

'Why? Are you planning to meet Carola?'

'I may.'

'You said that was over. That's why I'm here.'

'Oh,' he said vaguely. 'Promises made under pressure.'

'What does she think? Does she know I'm here, spending three days with you? That I met you at the airport. What the hell does she think?'

'She doesn't know. She thinks I'm arriving at the end of the week, when you return to the country.'

'I shall tell her.'

Van ripped his address book from a pile of papers behind him. She had spotted it there earlier and had registered its existence. There were many numbers for Carola. London, New York, Italy. Johann pressed his hand over the telephone but she kicked him away. She would go out and do it from a call-box, she said, if he persisted in thwarting her. She dialled the London number, recently added to the list, and Carola's voice answered after only two rings. It was deep and gloomy.

'It's Vanessa here,' she said. 'Vanessa Langford. I'm in Kennington with Johann. He arrived in London today. I met him at the airport and am spending three days with him. On

Friday he plans to swop me for you. Then, later in the month he plans to swop you for me again. I just rang to make sure that this suits you.'

There was a moan at the other end. Van rang off.

'By the way,' Johann told her, 'I bought you a present in Florence.' He minded nothing. Crazed with frustration and sadness, she howled at her inability to handle this weak man.

With shaky hands and swollen eyes, she slowly untied the little packet he had handed her. It had been gift-wrapped in a fashionable Florentine shop which specialised in objects made from marbled and decorative paper. Inside was a small collection of objects. A box, two pencils and a note-book. Inside the box were two alabaster eggs, presumably hewn and shaped in Volterra. Her eye was caught by a similarly wrapped packet half hidden behind the lamp. It was a different shape, smaller and more romantic looking, the wrapping of a paler, softer colour. She would destroy it when his back was turned.

A day or two earlier a letter had come for her in an unknown handwriting. The post-mark was a Sydney one and she opened it with curiosity. It was from Cheryl, the bright-eyed girl she had met at her niece's wedding. It said:

Dear Vanessa,

I feel awful. I guess I put my foot in it at the wedding. I have heard since of your attachment to Johann. I went through that mill myself and badly want to help you. Listen to me. I do not believe Johann is capable of love. What he calls love is a kind of temporary hectic flush that has nothing to do with behaviour. I know how terribly hard it is to break off with him. One keeps thinking there is something there, that these hints of generosity and sweetness imply something. But they don't really. At his centre is a radical emptiness. I don't know whether its causes are psychological or moral, but I do know he is a danger to people like you who are decent and capable of genuine love – who expect – being normal – reciprocity and responsibility. But it's like expecting a legless man to walk; perhaps he can come up with a kind of wooden-legged dance, but it has nothing of reality about it. Being with Johann is like being a spy; one feels one's finger on the pulse of life, somehow, and however sordid that life is, coming in from it would be a terrible let-down. Forgive me if my tone sounds tough. After all I don't know you but I have heard about you from your brother. You don't deserve a creature like Johann to eat up your life.

It was a kind letter. She should take Cheryl's advice. If only she could.

Johann claimed a business engagement the following day but promised to be back to take her to a play that evening. He left her, weak and mystified, in his bed. She picked up the romantic-looking parcel from behind a lamp and slipped it into her suitcase. Then, wandering about the house, she thought of how many times she had been alone there, having let herself in by the key on the string, and how little tempted she had been to pry. Now it was the opposite. She went to the file marked 'Correspondence' and untied the ribbon binding it together. Out they fell; not only her letters but many others in a more flowery, feminine hand than her own. They had been filed in order of arrival, sometimes one or more from each of them arriving on the same day throughout the summer. She took one out of its envelope. It was signed 'Carola'. The name was surrounded with kisses. Reading back, it said:

Only twenty-four hours until I see you again. Have a thrilling evening with Mrs L. of the massive interlect.

Perhaps he had told her that theirs was only an affair of the mind. Or had they simply colluded and mocked her? She remembered the dark surreal figures who had borne down on her during her black days. That was more likely. Why should Carola have known that he was dining with her, Van, when she herself knew nothing of his evenings with Carola? She worked it out. That had been written shortly after she had put him on the train loaded with vegetables and primroses stolen from her garden. Not long after he had passed out at the bottom of her staircase and her children had carted him to bed.

Caught in the net of animal jealousy, she placed the letter on his desk. Methodically she underlined the word 'interlect' and put a little 'sp' for spelling in the margin; she was a school-teacher. Then she wrote a note.

We thought we could trust each other but we couldn't.

How could she be in this fix? Days ahead, knowing the extent of his treachery and loving him to a point from which she could not return. Unused to using the telephones of others, she hesitated before ringing a friend who scooped her up, helped her out with her luggage containing Carola's gift-wrapped present. She was put to bed in a child's room in the friend's house, decorated by a frieze of dancing animals. She huddled, screwing up her body as tightly as she could, and slept after a fashion. In the night she woke and dialled his number. He had been asleep but was ready to talk.

'Van,' he said, 'darling. I'll explain. By the way. About Carola's spelling. Evelyn Waugh couldn't spell you know. It has nothing to do with intelligence.'

'Johann'.

'We must meet. I lied in order to keep you. Surely that must satisfy you, for Christ's sake. Why else should I have lied?'

'Perhaps you wanted to use my house.'

'God Almighty! It's a ghastly little house. There are a million places far nicer where I could have gone. I went there because of you. I wanted to be with you. I still do.'

She rang off and cried aloud on the stairs, grabbing her way to bed.

After that she suffered from a sort of inflammation of the mind; a pitiless sore which entered her limbs. Every time the telephone rang it was a dart under her skin. Her voice became shrill and wavery, and she feared for her life and her sanity.

One afternoon she went to the Kennington house. It was the second time she had called on Johann unexpectedly. If only that first time she had kissed the toad instead of him.

She was let in by a boy, stripped to the waist. He had been in the garden unblocking a gutter. She had interviewed him months before when Johann needed a jobbing gardener. It had been part of the contract that he should keep the patch tidy in spite of the cats.

The boy was pleased to see Van again, assuming that, having engaged his services, she would be around more often. With his crippling hangovers, Johann was a surly employer. He said:

'Kraesel's out. Gone to the doctor, he said. Earache, I believe. If you ask me it's a bit of something else as well.' She looked about.

She tucked a note under the Magimix. 'Why not still your little willy in here.' Then she went upstairs, sat on the duvet, and wrote at frantic speed.

'My darling one. What an awful time you must be having. I know that type of woman. You are sweet to confide in me and ask for my help. What a baby you were to get yourself into such a muddle. A blue baby. Of course I will help you out of it. I understand and rejoice that you should love me as you do. Let her down gently, as you suggest yourself. Same place. Same time. All my love. Van.'

This she hid where she knew he would never find it; on the side of the bed she had always occupied. In her memory he seldom crossed to that part of the room. Carola would be bound to see it.

Then she went to the shelf where he kept his files and plucked out the one marked correspondence; his trophy box. She called to the boy.

'Don't say I came. I've left a surprise and I don't want him to guess.'

At home she opened the file. Carola's letter, the one with the spelling correction in the margin, had been returned to its envelope and replaced, in correct order, next to her own as it had been when she first discovered it.

She dialled Johann's number.

Two purrs and then the rebuff of a click. The answering machine at work. Johann's voice spoke on tape, low and unchaste. She might have been anyone.

'Hello. Johann Kraesel here. I'm afraid I can't answer your call at the moment.' He made it so obvious. Clearly he was on the lavatory or slamming someone in the next room under the duvet.

Why couldn't he say, pure and simple, that he was out?

# *Chapter*
## IV

Anguish brought self-importance. She was unique. Straight and haughty, she walked with her shoulders back. Ladies from the village gathered in her sitting-room. The fete was drawing near and Muriel Bush, the vicar's wife, arranged with mastery a fortnightly sewing-bee. They stitched together, covering coat-hangers and stuffing cushions to sell on the sundries stall. Van stabbed with her needle at a length of felt, transforming it into a draught protector shaped as a dachshund, mournful and elongated. They talked of royalty; never of politics or cash. Muriel said, 'Who's going to keep this group together when Basil retires? I've been the live wire up to now.' She looked at Van. Perhaps that's what she was. A live wire.

In need of money after the extra expense of Johann, she turned to her walls.

'Roman Charity' would have to go. An ancient canvas, encrusted and dirty, hung in the dining-room between french windows leading to the garden. A prisoner with matted hair rapaciously sucking at the breast of his daughter from between bars. The story was half-hidden by swollen excrescences, bubbles and warts. However, the wary expression in the melting eyes of the provider shone through the rotten condition of the painting. It might have a value.

She sat alone in the auction room. It was an Old Masters sale and 'Roman Charity' was labelled 'Lot 141'. There was a long time to wait. If it reached its reserve her love would be requited. The bidding varied, sometimes leaping in sums of a hundred pounds, then, for no good reason, jumping in twenties. It was as formless as her existence. The auctioneer leant forward in his lectern. Grey-suited, an open mouthed assistant sat at his side taking notes. The chairs stood on rugs with labels attached.

Everything was up for sale. The bidders, heads nodding, pencils twitching, in training for a chorus dance. It was a mime show. What if they started to bid with throbbing members? Raising and lowering them, bursting buttons; she thought of Johann. Some of the bidders were women. She wondered how they were feeling.

In good times she would have enjoyed taking a friend, sharing the excitement. Mary perhaps? They would have lunched together afterwards, drinking a bottle of wine. The painting failed to reach its reserve. It was a flop.

Johann's defensive habit of attentive silence frightened her when she thought back. Perhaps he had been drunker more often than she had realised. A man with a missing cylinder. How could she get him back? Only by forgiving him. His selfishness was infinite.

Promptly he answered a long letter she wrote to him.

'Thank God we are friends. Good girl. Meet me on the steps of the National Gallery and we will lunch at a Soho restaurant. I know I have treated you badly but I love you very much and we will be best friends in the world. You have a great hold over me and, if you show enormous effort of will, you will get me in the end – for what I'm worth.'

Reeling both with hope and with rage at his conceit and off-hand advice, she arrived on the steps of the National Gallery at one o'clock, dressed in her best and in a state of exciteable ferment. At the restaurant table, sitting at right-angles to each other, their four eyes met. He passed her a new, slim paperback book.

Half numb with love, she fingered and opened it. It was a collection of poems. *The Whitsun Weddings*, by Philip Larkin.

Johann snatched it back and fumbled through the pages, then, presenting her with the page of his finding, read aloud from the last verse of a poem called 'Wild Oats'.

'Do you think this describes me?

"Parting, after above five
Rehearsals, was an agreement
That I was too selfish, withdrawn,
And easily bored to love."'

She asked: 'Which rehearsal is this?'
Then their lips touched one another's. A waiter asked if they
were father and daughter. She was terribly hot and wondered
at his surmise: how incestuous they must appear to be. That
morning, she had dressed, as for a great occasion, in a striped
silk suit. The top half of the outfit was a blouse of sorts with an
open neck that could either be buttoned or left undone. She
had left it open and under it was wearing a blue polo-necked
jumper. Now she was hot with wine, excitement and the
closeness of others. She removed the silk blouse and began to
pull the jumper towards her head, exposing her brassiere and a
little pink rose between the cups. Johann was horrified.
'You're mad. You can't do that. Put it back. Good girl.'
Having obeyed, she smarted and wished that nothing had
happened to cloud the bliss of the meeting. Soon he forgot and
talked, frenziedly of his work. Half his belongings, clothes,
books and papers were still in her Tuscan house. He would
have to return there very soon. The business that had,
ostensibly, brought him back to London had taken longer than
intended.
'Johann. Our holiday. Could we after all? I'm not in love
with you any more – at least I don't think I am. Couldn't we
have our holiday together?'
He looked at her.
'Nothing I'd like more. My dearest friend in the world. No
more rows. No more problems. Friends forever.'
'Are you happy?'
'Desperately.'
They kissed in the street before she turned and ran, happy as
on the day of their first amorous encounter.

'Ring me,' he called after her.

They talked that evening. After seeing her depart, running ecstatically away from him, Johann had called in at a wedding party.

Fluent and friendly, he outlined their plans.

'I shall go ahead,' he said. 'I have to work in Venice for a day or two. You go straight to the house. We will have some days together there as we always intended to do. Then we will travel slowly through France. Nothing has changed. Presumably you will go by car.'

'Yes,' she said. 'Then we will be able to bring your books back.'

'Excellent. Good.'

He was to open the house, light fires, air beds and prepare for her arrival. Dinner, he told her, would be ready and on the table the following Tuesday evening.

She told him where to find hot-water-bottles, in a blue enamel-lidded bin, protecting them from damp, in the kitchen.

'I shall take a train from Florence to Lucca,' he told her, 'and then a taxi to the house. I shall get there a day before your arrival so as to have it ready.' He made a suction noise down the wire. She was being kissed.

Melissa and Polly would be at school once again. Van rang Uncle Jim's number and asked if he could take them out on their free day.

'Of course, darling. Any time. It'll do you good to go to Italy. See plenty of Charles and Henry and don't do anything that I wouldn't do.'

# Chapter
## V

Now it was all behind her. Carola, the opening of her lover's letters, the panic of pain and the fears for her sanity. The Tuscan house shone luminous in her mind's eye as a fire in a grate, glowing and full of colour. She let her poetic imagination fancy light streaming from every window, sparks from the chimney, candles burning in the angles of rooms, boiling water from rusty taps, and steam from Johann's cooking. It became a campfire in her heart, shutting out painful memories. The bed, the one with the ill-fitting mattress, sagging from the extra weight of covering as winter approached, warmed with hot-water-bottles from the blue enamel bin, would rise like dough to welcome her.

Together they would spend nights there and the mysteries of her tortured months would be solved. She would pander to his quirks, dress as a nurse even, and bath him with Dettol; take his temperature in a near-darkened room and look intently at her watch whilst taking note of his pulse. There would be further treats. She would summon Rupert and Lucy for one night at least. Make him feel popular, part of the world. In London, on her way to Dover, she stopped at a chemist's shop and bought a medium-sized bottle of Dettol. The transaction made her laugh. She had never entered an unorthodox world before.

By mid-day she had boarded the boat and taken a seat by the window. She looked at the sea and at the seagulls, almost swan-sized. With her she had an anthology of American verse which she read with concentration to steady her happiness. A short poem by Emily Dickinson caught her eye. She copied the first verse onto a piece of paper and tucked it into her wallet alongside travelling money.

'Wild Nights! Wild Nights!
Were I with thee,
Wild Nights would be
Our Luxury!'

The wild nights before her and the flickering heat of her
Tuscan retreat were beckoning, carrying her forward, with the
long journey by road in her inadequate car, much complained
of by Johann, still ahead.

In Calais she fastened her seat-belt and hoped it would
protect her for the whole of her holiday, not only when in the
driver's seat. Propelled by the bright magnet of her destination, she drove for many miles that day, to Fontainebleau,
where she stopped and slept until the morning.

It was a great awakening. She was strong enough to do it,
strapped in by her seat-belt, her foot hard down on the
accelerator. Beside her she kept a bag of apples. She ate one of
these from time to time, casting the cores, airily, from the
window.

It would be about seven hundred miles, all in one day, but
without hitches – it could be done. Nothing would prevent
her.

It was a little after mid-day when she drove under the Mont
Blanc. Half way through the tunnel there was an illuminated
sign to tell southbound travellers that they had driven over the
line and were now in Italy. The worst was over. She was in the
right country. People drive around within the boundaries of
one country all the time. The challenge had been met and
reality was entering her soul. Perhaps he would be cooking. At
any rate he would have chosen the ingredients for their first
supper together. Maybe, already in a kimono, he would be
peeling tomatoes and chopping herbs.

At five in the afternoon she arrived in Genoa. By then she
had been at the wheel for ten remorseless hours. Her hands
were still steady, but her bright destination was slipping from
her mind's focus. The warm and golden image of the
beckoning Tuscan house began to fade. Here the road, rising

above the port, became a ribbon hanging in air, linking the motorways. Driving along it she was suspended, as though over the sea.

Van felt giddy and took a firm grip on the steering-wheel. Darkness and drops of rain started to fall. Her energy began to dribble away and melt into tiredness. A relentless number of tunnels opened up before her.

The tussle started and the image was gone. It was a question of tackling the journey piece by piece. Yard by yard almost. Oncoming cars and lorries were dragons breathing fire. Her belt was uncomfortable and she groped for cigarettes. The apples were finished and a weakness, from hunger, attacked her. The rain came heavily, too fast for the power of her windscreen wipers. She drove forward, very slowly now, for fear of losing control.

Then at last she was on familiar ground. She left the last lap of the motorway, paying her way out of it, very wearily, at the ALT station. Her body ached. Her hands and feet trembled.

Soon it was home territory. She passed the plumber's house, painted pink. It looked like a birthday cake and had plastic pineapples perched on pillars at each side of the gate. Then she turned the corner between the butcher's shop and the general store and started to wind up into her hill.

The image returned. The hour was right. It was nearly seven — time for a bath before Johann's culinary masterpieces. It was cold, but the image remained.

At the bottom of her drive, she stopped, unfastened her belt, and stepped out onto the rough road. The house was out of sight, though within shouting distance. It was still raining. She shook herself, brushing away the ash from cigarettes and the odd pip or stalk from the apples she had eaten. Then she cleaned her teeth, after a fashion, and doused herself with scent from a bottle intended for Carola. The romantic-looking parcel she had stolen from Kennington had contained two bottles. Desert Nights, this one was called. The other she had lost.

The tiredness left her body and she turned up her own drive, straining for a view of the glowing house.

There was no light. He must have shuttered it up well. What a fuss-pot. Then the final halt. The house was dead. No sparks from the chimney, no light through the cracks. The door into the kitchen, the one they nearly always used, tightly locked. No key in the key-hole. She called his name and ran around the house beating on the windowpanes. The outdoor table was covered in a plastic sheet weighed down at each corner by a log, protecting it from the winter. Leaves from the Virginia creeper, now a reddish brown, dropped upon it.

There was a spare key under a brick by a tap in the wall behind the house. She had left her car lights on and they guided her to the dilapidated area. They key was there, huge and heavy, in the dark corner. The lock was stiff and it took the little energy left inside her to turn it and then to push open the door. She was in the kitchen. With a flick of her finger the light was on.

The fridge door was open wide showing dark emptiness within. It gave out an acrid smell, which combined with a whiff of escaping gas. It was perishingly cold. She lifted the lid of the blue enamel bin and looked down at her store of hot-water-bottles. They were there, not in use. The water-heater had not been turned on, beds were unmade, the house was dank and deserted.

Beside the abandoned fireplaces, log baskets were empty. There was a layer of fluffy mould on the brickwork in the hall, like a thin sprinkling of snow. She sat, heavily, on an arm-chair. It could not possibly be. She spoke staunchly to herself, out loud.

'You unutterable idiot. Nothing ever has been or ever could be right with Johann. That is the nature of him.'

Alone and still, she sat in the cold without a telephone and without the strength to reach one. There was a noise, a faint pattering without. She ran to the door. All was well. He had come. But it was a false alarm. A family of wild boar that hovered in the hills must have decided to call.

A bottle of grappa, half full, stood on the marble-topped table in the dining-room. After one gulp there was warmth inside her and she filled a tumbler to brimming point. Then her eye was caught by a stack of cylinders, about thirty in all, randomly piled together like spillikins, on the dining table, rolled-up editions of various newspapers addressed to Johann. He had ordered them to be sent to him when laying his first schemes and they had not been cancelled. Perfect for lighting a fire. She made a wig-wam in the fireplace. It was a new thing, she had read about it, turning paper into logs.

She sat beside the flames, sipping from the tumbler, surrounded by mice droppings and souvenirs from the summer. Johann's bus timetable was on the stool and a bunch of artificial flowers he had bought for her from the market in Siena.

Then came a whirlwind: the shrill Italian voice of her neighbour, the one from down below whose telephone they used in emergencies.

'Signora!' They embraced. Words tumbled from her lips. There was a telephone message. The German gentleman had rung. He was with Rupert and Lucy, her friends, in Florence. He had borrowed one of their cars and would be with her in an hour. Together they set the house to rights. Her neighbour, Bruna, legs bandaged to enclose varicose veins, ran through the rain down the hill where she raided her own larder and returned, apron filled with provisions.

In exactly one hour it was the house of her image.

Fires, candles, cooking and light. It took a while for the water to heat. It was a risk to embark on a bath. She wanted to be down, dressed and ready, re-armed in Carola's scent, when he drove up in Rupert's second car. It wouldn't do to be caught in a bath-cap in the chilly bathroom. An hour from Florence was an optimistic assessment, particularly in this weather, and it was imperative that she should look her best; shake off fatigue and the effects of grappa. For a moment she brooded. Why should Johann be with Rupert and Lucy? She had planned to lay them on as part of her treat. Now he had spoilt it. Nonetheless he was on his way, and the Dettol bottle was already unpacked.

A simple supper was prepared and the table laid. Bruna left her with smiles and kisses after filling hot-water-bottles and tucking them into Van's bed. The time was half past eight. Little had been lost. Her body was alive, resilient. She wondered at its power.

It was quiet in the house. Van went upstairs and looked into the room which Johann had occupied. Tables were heaped with books and she could see his typewriter, the one she had taken to Bethnal Green. The wardrobe, a roomy, built-in one leading from the bathroom into the passage, housed his clothes. Two fine kimonos, side by side on hangers, fell in the shape of his body alongside other garments, all new-looking and well kept. Above these, on a shelf, were three pairs of shoes, one of them very stout. A black leather suitcase with flapping straps was tucked away under the kimonos on the floor. Also on the shelf, beside the shoes, was a pile of shirts, a tie or two and a tweed cap. Soon he would be wearing them. Nine o'clock came. And then ten o'clock.

Johann was a bad driver, uncoordinated. The dinner she had prepared had congealed. Sitting, again, beside the fire she gulped at what remained of the grappa, still in a tumbler from the moment of Bruna's appearance. The hours passed. Eleven o'clock. Midnight.

There was a bend in the staircase, a brick-laid platform. This, too, was covered in fluffy white mould. She rubbed her face into it, grazing her nose. Pulling at the stair rail, manoeuvring her body round the bend, her heart beat in her throat. The door to Johann's cupboard was still open from her reconnoitre there and her eye was caught by the brightness of a robe.

Even in her condition of drunken helplessness, she was capable of consecutive thought and wondered, once again, at the changing capacities of her body. Now she was standing, unhooking hangers from the rail and hurtling garments, one on top of the other, onto the landing floor. Shoes, ties and kimonos piled high as a human form. It took three journeys to transport them, hangers and all, to the fireplace below. The flimsy cloth of the kimonos barely more than flickered before reducing to a black ooze. The woolly texture of jumpers and cap gave out black smoke and it was some time before they, too, subsided into dark ash. The shoes were more challenging and she had to light two candles before resurrecting a flame strong enough to lick them up.

All the while she cursed him for reducing her to this.

It had been a long day, starting a country away. Her hopes had been high, dashed, high again and then destroyed, like jagged peaks on a temperature chart.

On the floor, beside the remains of his clothes, she passed out.

Cruelly, her unconsciousness did not last. The cold brought her round in the early hours of morning. Then rigors, uncontrolled tremors, took over her feeble form. Her teeth chattered and she could not rise. Half awake, she wondered what had happened to his clothes.

It must have been mid-day when he found her there. She was relieved to see him clad. It had occurred to her that from now on he would be naked, whatever the weather.

He sat on a sofa, beside where she lay, and held his head in his hands.

'Van,' he said. 'Van darling. Why are you on the floor?'

'Why didn't you come?'

'I got plastered. I went to see Rupert and Lucy. In fact we met up in Florence and they suggested I should go home with them and borrow their car.'

'You knew I was here. Did they?'

'Well. Only a day late. No, they didn't. Why the fuss?'

'I think I've burnt your clothes.'

Electrified, he asked, 'What do you mean? What do you mean you think? You must know. You can't burn clothes and then not know if you've done it or not. Van, I warned you earlier, you are mad. Completely bonkers. Mad, Van. You are mad.'

'Make me sane. Take me to bed. Help me please.'

She saw him now, white and waxy as she had seen him before, sagging cheeks and shifting eyes. She loved and wanted him with the strength of a goddess. He helped himself to a drink. There was still a supply, except of the grappa, left from his previous sojourn. Then, fearful, he ran to his room calling out, 'My books. Are they safe?'

She could hear him, in the cupboard, swearing and wondering at the emptiness of it.

'Those shoes, Van,' he called to her, 'the stout ones with nails. Those, even you could not have burnt. It would take a month in an incinerator to burn those. Where are they?'

'I don't know.' Then she knew, remembered, and they had, eventually, curled up and dissolved into her pyre.

The rain had stopped and the day was sunny. Side by side they sat on the stone table, ill and unhappy. Sadly their power was unequally divided. He had the means, then and there, to ease her of all torment whereas she, the underdog, had no spells to cast upon him.

'Van,' he said. 'After what happened last night you must understand something. I can never make love to you again. Sleep in the same bed, yes, that perhaps, but never again will we be lovers.' To her it was everything. Perhaps to him it had never meant more than riding a bicycle.

There was a scuffle below. Visitors approached. No daughters were there to give warning. In place of puffing complaints, chanting, sonorous and low, could be heard. A scanty procession turned the corner coming into view. The dense frame of Father Gobbi, priest of the village, rounded the twist at the top of the drive. He was shadowed by acolytes, dressed in white, swinging in unison with the chant, incense in filigree balls attached to black ribbons. They were there to bless the house. Could it be that somebody had tipped them off? No sanctifying agent could help it now.

Van went forward to shake each by the hand. The Father beamed on her. It was not the season for this type of blessing but the priest, greedy for his parish, pounced on the knowledge that the house was occupied. Every room would be made part of the symbolic act. In the sitting-room incense curled, following smoke from the pyre up the chimney. Then the dining-room; chanting amongst empty wine bottles. The portly priest led his followers up the staircase, treading lightly on fluffy mould; then the bedroom. Prayers muttered in Johann's bedroom came too late. No need, now, to protect it from sin. There are sins of omission. Perhaps Father Gobbi could lend a hand there. A passing blessing, a blown kiss, was extended to the empty wardrobe. Van thought back to the first day, the day of the telephone call from Hamburg, and of Uncle Jim's warning. 'Don't touch him with a barge-pole.' Now the tables were turned.

Begging Johann to remain where he was, for a day or two at least, she drove away in the sunshine in search of help. She was loath to disturb James and Henry.

Taking it slowly, partly from shame at being unheralded, and partly from road weariness, she arrived at the gate of their walled-in house.

James was outside inspecting a load of gravel that had been delivered that morning and deposited in the wrong spot. He recognised her car, brightly coloured and battered, in an instant. From her seat she saw something wonderful. A grin was spreading, lovingly, over his face. He turned and called to the house.

'Henry. The most marvellous thing has happened. Vanessa is here. Mercy. How unexpected!'

Henry kissed her and said 'What on earth is the matter? You'd better stay here. James will make some tea and we'll go together and make up a bed for you.'

She shook and cried, but they remained perfectly calm and said that she had better tell them about it, that was if she wanted to.

'I can't. You will despise me for ever. That I couldn't bear.'

'Of course we won't.' They spoke together, the same words at the same moment.

She lived it again; the drive, the rain falling on the Genoa flyover, the cars like dragons and the innumerable tunnels.

Then the clothes. Johann's clothes going up in smoke. Again they spoke together but, this time, they said different things.

James said, 'I think it's a miracle you didn't cut his balls off with a carving knife.'

Henry said, 'You've never done a better thing. His clothes were perfectly appalling. I think you've done him, and everybody else, a good turn.'

Laughing, her industrious friends decided, probably for the first time since their venture began, to allow themselves an unpremeditated day off work. Henry said that she would have to return to her house, not that day but the next, and that they would accompany her. They did not trust her an inch. Johann must be sent packing. Not that he had much to pack. They would put him onto a night train at Pisa.

'What about his books? I spared them at least.'

'Those, I'm afraid, you must take home with you when you go. That would be the decent thing to do. You can drop them at one of his drinking clubs. But not before you have had a holiday here with us.'

James and Henry could see that her shaken nerves were not equal to renewed torture which would, without any doubt, be inflicted on them were she to have further truck with Johann. There was room in their well ordered lives for compassion and correctitude. She was, now, keeping good company. The very best. She recognised this with satisfaction. With Johann it had been a cold bath from which it was impossible to extract her body. Had someone, say, turned on a hot tap, she might, perhaps, have found it easier to jump out.

# *Chapter*
## VI

---

Lying that night in the spare bedroom at her friends' house, she found the tips of her fingers and thumbs were numb.

'That will be from shock,' James told her at breakfast. 'It's well known. It will pass.'

Sitting up in bed she sipped from a cup of camomile tea. Henry brought her an old dressing-gown in which to wrap herself.

For the first time in many years she thought of the dead husband who had treasured her. That is not to say that he did not, frequently, slip into her thoughts. But she would never allow him to rest there.

What misery he would have suffered had he known of her state of mind. The pain, in the early days after his death, had been unendurable. A doctor she knew had told her that it was possible to blank out certain areas of the mind. Very often this had to be done, he told her, in the case of intolerable bereavement. One day, he said, it would be all right and she would be able to think of Martin calmly. This moment had never come. She had continued to shut him out, rearing the children and holding fast to the dilapidated properties he had left her. He had ended his own life in the final stages of an incurable illness. The letter he left behind told of his love for all of them but of his hatred of his own body, racked with disease. It had been an act of courage, she now saw, not of cowardice. At the time she had believed he had deserted her.

Low and wretched, with every nerve on edge, she tried to dream of better times, of journeys she had made. Bolivia was the oddest country. If only she could conjure up the memory of it and concentrate. She cherished a notion that all would be well if she could recreate good memories from the past.

She had gone to Bolivia with Martin, soon after they were married and before the children were born. Martin had said 'It's now or never.' Together they had been to many countries, been buffeted about in tiny aeroplanes flown by crazy pilots. She must focus on one country at a time. A country a day might do the trick.

They had left early for Lima airport. They had to fly over the Andes in an unpressurised plane. Rubber tubes were provided for each passenger. You could either stick them up your nose or into your mouth, whichever you preferred. Van wanted to ask which decision the passenger before her had made, but Martin said, 'Don't be absurd. Stick it up your nose. You might go blue if you don't and I'm not having that.'

They dipped into tropical air pockets and Van hid her head in her hands. Martin ran his fingers through her hair and looked out of the window. He told her that the landscape was dusty brown and that they would soon be there.

The air was thin. Several hundred soldiers goose-stepped their way across the runway.

Her plan was working. It could have been yesterday.

At the airport they were besieged by rat-faced men clawing for luggage tickets, soliciting the job of carrying their bags. Driving from the airport plateau, they passed a steep bend in the road and looked down on La Paz. At the bend, buckled out of recognition, was a car on the end of a pole, warning reckless drivers against hurtling over the unfenced road onto the glittering tin roofs of the town, thousands of feet below.

Now Van's head was filling with images.

Jagged snow-capped mountains, lunar and thrilling; Martin was beside her, red-headed, a proper copper-knob, laughing at her ways. All about her were Indians, women tidily dressed in bunchy colourful skirts and shawls, with long pigtails and bowler hats perched on their heads. They were everywhere, crouching by the road, furiously spinning on their hand-looms, crawling in and out of low mud huts.

Martin never stopped looking things up.

'Goat's penis for dinner,' he told her. 'It's a great speciality here.'

They bumped over cobbled roads to the Hotel Crillon. Martin had looked that up too. It had been built by Patino as a peace-offering to La Paz, he told her. Guilt-ridden by the fortune he had made from Bolivian tin, the Crillon was his eccentric method of making amends. Van told Martin to stop looking things up.

He said, 'Wait for this. We must expect to find blood pouring out of our ears at this altitude.' They weren't sure, but it might well have been goat's penis that they ate that night. Packs of wild dogs yodelled outside, and they slept fitfully on hard iron beds. The bath water was brown and large spiders crept over the side of the tub. In the morning they both had headaches. They peered, laughing, into each other's ears but found no sign of blood.

They explored the town. Martin, book in hand, guided her to the unsavoury black magic street.

Van, in the spare room at her friends' house, cigarette in hand, willed the memories to take over.

She was passing stall after stall of dried llama foetuses. The Indians built them into the walls of their houses to bring good luck. She was encircled by skinned rats, prepared for human consumption, pig foetuses, brightly-coloured sweets, raw drugs and wild-looking dogs.

Martin had telephoned a friend of his mother's, Mrs Whip; she was the wife of an English banker there. They called on her. She and her husband had taken their flat furnished. Not a stick of furniture had been moved during their three-year stay. Mrs Whip was around forty. She had thin hair. Something was wrong. She barely noticed they were there. A signed photograph of Prince Philip and a letter addressed to Harrods lying in the hall made Van want to cry. Mrs Whip led them upstairs to a dirty sitting-room. After a glass of sherry she talked slowly and drearily about the altitude and the effect it had on health.

'It's not so much the immediate effects,' she said, 'it's the long term ones. One's nerves go you know, and one's temper.'

Her talk was of pills, sedatives, injections and headaches. The dogs were rabid and the people dishonest. Martin was trying not to laugh. Mrs Whip offered to drive them back to their hotel, only a few minutes away. 'It would be better if you could take a taxi but you can't get them here.'

Mrs Whip's energy was aroused. She had lost some important keys. They couldn't leave the house until they were found. Van and Martin joined in the search. It was hopeless looking for something they had never seen in the house of someone they hardly knew. The nightmare lasted half an hour. Mrs Whip gave Van a torch and told her to look under the sofa. The keys belonged to a drinks cupboard and she couldn't trust her maid not to get at it when she was out. She had lost a bottle of port the year before. It wasn't certain which maid it had been, since they each blamed it on one another. Anyway port was useless there, too heavy for the digestion.

The keys were found in a suitcase. Later Martin discovered excellent reasons for Mrs Whip's jangled state of nerves. Her husband had been reduced to a gibbering wreck by the altitude, deciding that La Paz was the centre of the universe. There was almost nothing to do at the bank, but he started work at eight in the morning, continued frenziedly through-out the day, chain-smoking and never stopping for lunch. Apparently Mrs Whip sometimes gigglingly spoke of divorce at cocktail parties, but was too beaten down to take action.

Van had thought how weak Mrs Whip was allowing outside circumstances to disrupt the intricate balance of her mind.

Another time they would try a sunnier climate. Panama or Brazil. In Brazil the children had loved Martin's hair, sidling up to him and extracting strands. Van had loved it too.

The pain of remembering was worse than reality, if reality it was, this cavity she was in.

They were boarding a jolly little train with an observation car, and a five-hour journey across Bolivia to Lake Titicaca ahead. Martin was proud of her.

'Thank God you're not like Mrs Whip, Van. You're the sanest girl I've ever known.'

They lunched on Mackintosh toffees, holding hands.

She was being sucked back.

Looking out at elegant Indian women, faces unlined, sitting erect, never wasting a moment. Frantically they were knitting or spinning, many of them with fingerless hands thanks, perhaps, to syphilis or leprosy. Donkeys, cows and snortling long-haired pigs. Dogs, crazed with boredom yelping after the train. Distances were confusing. You could put your hand out of the train window to touch the bright clothes of a peasant, possibly many miles away; illusions caused by thin air.

If the air were thinner still she would be able to touch Martin's hair. Now grown up, the children in Brazil might still have some strands.

Tomorrow she would try again.

They boarded the train to take them across the lake. It was the prettiest boat she had ever seen. Built in Hull in 1905 (Martin had looked it up) it had been carried in sections from the coast by mule and was a masterpiece of Edwardian design. Their minute cabin was exquisite; white wrought-iron beds, one on top of the other. The walls were white matchboarding, the ceiling fine white panelling, the carved cornice intricate and the brass work dazzling. She had never been so happy. There were brass coat-hooks, light switches, complicated bolts and beautiful fitted candlesticks. The dining-room gripped her mind. Buttoned velvet sofas ran along each side of the room.

Brass rods held velvet curtains, faded fringes and tassels. In Puccara, the other side of the lake, upturned pigs lay dead in gutters. Indians, still inscrutable in bowler hats, relieved themselves of excrement; huge dollops. They bought a pottery bull. It was heavy. Terrible to carry. Now it was on the shelf of her kitchen dresser, in England. The memory of its weight was with her. Martin had carried it for the most part but she had taken a turn once or twice.

She would take it to the garden and bury it on her return.

Johann. He had made her live once again with her emotions. His magnetism had tugged her like a suction pump, out of her buried self, but she had fallen into the wrong hands. Perhaps one day she would bless him as a stepping-stone to better things.

On the following day they went, all three of them, back to her house in search of Johann. He was upstairs, typing in his bedroom, delighted to see them. Henry said, 'We think you should go back to London tonight. Vanessa will return the car you borrowed from her friends and we will fetch her from there. She will take your books back to England for you. Perhaps you should pack.'

'Nothing to pack. Hem, hem. Nothing to pack nothing in. Van, did you burn my suitcase? The black leather one with straps?'

She remembered having burnt that too. It had been the hardest thing to dispose of and had occupied the entire space of the fireplace. It had needed a lot of kicking and poking before it would lodge in the flames.

'It doesn't really matter if she burnt it since you have nothing to put in it,' James said. 'Take a plastic bag. We'll run you to the station.'

Johann, like a bull towards the end of a bloody fight, was diminished. His magnificent body was heavy and lifeless. Again Van wondered if his arms were not a little long. Out of proportion.

They put him on a train at seven o'clock. First he had to buy postcards; then write on them. He asked Van if she would post them for him. He wanted them to be stamped in Italy. Then she saw that he had barely registered the drama through which they had passed. Neither now nor at any other time. Cheryl had been right. There was, indeed, a radical emptiness. He had suffered mild irritation at the loss of his belongings but no real surprise and no understanding of the reason for it all. Such things had probably happened to him many times before.

Vanessa went alone to visit Santa Zita, patron saint of serving maids. The shrivelled remains of her heroine lay, gaudily decked, in a glass box on top of the altar in a side chapel at the church of San Freddiano in Lucca, not far from the Piazzo del Anfiteatro.

When small, Melissa and Polly would climb onto the altar and press their noses into the glass of the box, eyes firm-set on the worm-bitten face. The antique skin was stretched, taut and yellow; nostrils hollow. On the ornamented lace of her frock a bunch of plastic flowers were strewn to remind worshippers of the miracle that saved the day. Zita, from the most impoverished of families, toiled as a serving maid in the castle of a tyrant in the hills above the town.

One day she gathered scraps, crumbs from the rich man's table, and filled her apron; a treat for her starving sisters. Leaving the castle, running across the field, she was spotted. The tyrant commanded her to let her apron fall. The punishment would be great. With quaking hands – still to be seen, warped and shrivelled in the glass case – she untied the knot. Out fell a bunch of flowers. She was saved. Van strained in an effort to pray. She must dwell on past happiness, record golden moments before the curse of Johann entered and invaded her system. Good memories would save her.

Mesmerised by her visit to the saint, Van sat for a while on the steps outside the cathedral portico beneath glistening mosaics. Many women had suffered troubles at the hands of rotters. Troubles, on paper, far worse than her own; irreversible tragedies.

Janey, for a start.

At the beginning they had set up house in London, in a Chelsea terrace, before Martin's mother died or, rather, before she began to think about dying, at which time they had to help her out of the old rectory and move into it themselves.

Van found housekeeping burdensome, particularly when the children were small or about to be born. One day the door bell rang. A timid mortal stood on the door-step. After looking at Van for a second, her glance slid towards the railings, then dropped to the ground. She said, very softly, 'I came about the job but I expect you've got somebody. It doesn't matter. Are you foreign?'

'No. I'm English. What did you think I was?'

She giggled. 'I'm ever so sorry. Do you think I'm cheeky? Aren't I awful? Are you pregnant?'

'Yes. Eight months.'

'Never mind. It's not your fault. I understand, I've got kids myself. Mary and Arthur. I love kids. Is it your first?'

'Yes, it is. I'm afraid I've found somebody to do the work. A lady from the block of flats. She won't clean shoes or do the ironing. Would you?'

'I don't mind what I do. I've had a rough life. You ask my neighbours. They'll tell you I've had a rough life.'

Van charmed, magnetised by her artlessness, asked her to come in and offered her a cigarette. Making vague reference to a husband, the girl said:

'But I'd rather not talk about him if you don't mind. He's a rotter. I've had a rotten life, I'm telling you. I've had some rotten jobs too. Are you religious?'

'Not particularly.'

'I am. I was brought up Catholic. I come from Sligo. It's a rotten religion. I like the Quakers. They're lovely. There's a Meeting House in Blythe Road. Do you know it? Society of Friends, it's called. You know — friends. Fancy me sitting here having a cigarette with you. I thought at first you were Italian

— you know, Italian. You look Italian with your hair. I am awful, aren't I?'

She said she would start work the following day.

When she'd gone Van crossed the road to the block of flats. She left a note for Mrs Williams, the lady she had engaged as cleaner the day before, telling her not to come since her predecessor had decided, after all, not to leave.

A week later the house was shining. Janey had polished every stick of it. Van felt she should have warned the house, gone from table to chair telling them in advance of the unusual treatment they were about to suffer, explaining it was for their own ultimate good.

The baby had been born and the house was snug and complete. Van fretted about the Jamaican midwife who had helped her through labour. They had hard lives.

When she emerged, she asked Martin, singlehearted and kind, 'How's everybody? How's Janey?' Martin said that he was anxious. She hadn't been in since Van took to her bed. He did a little shopping and walked off in the direction of the gasworks, beyond World's End. The houses in the street where Janey lived were dilapidated; number twelve more so than the rest. Janey's son, Arthur, opened the door to Martin and led him in without hestitation. He was a nice-looking boy, thin, fair and neatly dressed.

Janey's flat was on the first floor. It was well looked after. There was a different paper on each of the walls in the hall and the ceiling was painted sky-blue. The lino on the floor was patterned with pebbles, closely packed like a section of the beach. Arthur led Martin to a square room overlooking the street. Here they found Janey.

Martin said that they had been worried about her and that they had had a little daughter.

'Bless her soul. A little girl. Are you disappointed? Never mind. Here, aren't I dreadful? Sit down. I've been rotten. Else I'd have been in. Honestly. I've been really rotten. Anyone'll tell you. Go on, Arthur, you tell him how rotten I've been. It's no use asking those people downstairs. They're rotten too. Everybody's rotten in this street. Would you like to see the kitchen? I papered it myself. Honest I did, didn't I Arthur? He'll tell you straight.' Gloating, enraptured over the food Martin had brought her, Janey said, 'You shouldn't have done that honest. I feel dreadful letting you down this week. You know what I mean. Just this week like. Did she suffer a lot? I suffered when I had Mary and now look at her. She's a little monster. I chastise her all the time. They say you shouldn't chastise them but you have to, honestly. You know – chastise. You have to. They break your heart, kids do. Go on, Arthur. You tell him what Mary can be like.'

Van and Janey were sitting in the kitchen smoking cigarettes. Janey looked at the sink and said, 'Did you guess I was pregnant? You know – pregnant. Isn't it awful? It's that man. He's a brute. Anyone'll tell you. You ask Arthur and Mary. He's dreadful. A real rotter. That's it. Rotten. Rotten through and through.'

Van's head was in a spin. 'But Janey. Was it your husband?'

'That's right. It was him. Isn't it awful? We're separated. He left a couple of years ago. You know, separated. Honestly, I'm telling you straight. He walked out. You ask Arthur if his Dad walked out. He'll tell you straight.'

'What about the baby? I mean if you haven't seen him for two years.'

'I'm pregnant all right. Honest I am. Five months. Didn't you notice? That's it. He came to see the kids at Christmas. I didn't want to see him but he found out where we were. You can ask anyone. You ask Arthur and Mary if I didn't try to keep him out. I've had bad luck. I fall easy. You know, easy. Isn't it dreadful? He charged me. I didn't want anything to do with him. He just charged me. You should hear Mary poor kid. "Do you remember when he charged you?" she says. Honest she says that. "Do you remember when he charged you, Mum?" I'm adopting it out. I'm not bringing up another kid for that rotter.'

'Couldn't you have shouted for the neighbours? Even those dreadful people downstairs, surely they would have done something if they'd known you were actually being charged.' She said this awkwardly, never having heard the expression before.

'Not them. They wouldn't have lifted a finger. They're rotten. They know all about it. They say terrible things. They keep screaming that I'm a whore. That's it. Whore. You ask Mary if they don't keep screaming out that her Mum's a whore. That woman. She's the worst. "Whose is it?" she shouts that after me. I'm telling you straight. You ask Arthur. All the neighbours have started now except Paddy next door. He's decent, Paddy is. They'd never dare do it if there was a man about. That's it. They'd never dare. It's dreadful being on your own down there. It's a nice flat but I'd like to move. I've asked them down at the Friends if they can't get me out but they don't believe it's that bad. Honest they don't.'

Van asked her about the Quakers.

'They've fixed it. The Society of Friends. I'm going to St Stephen's to have it. I hope I don't suffer. I suffered with Mary. They never should have done it like that. They should have given me something. I'll get one of the Friends to go round and tell them to give me something – pills and that.'

'Are you really going to put it out for adoption?'

'I'm not keeping it. Not with the neighbours calling it a bastard and that. That's it. That's what they'd do. Call it a bastard and me a whore. Poor old Janey and her problems. You're ever so good to me. I was pleased with those clothes you gave me. I wore the suit last night. I can't wear it much longer though. Not in my condition. Honestly, it's the kids I feel for. It's dreadful for Arthur at school with his mum called a whore. But I'm not. Honest I'm not. He charged me and I fell easy. That's it. I'm telling you.'

Van, out of her depth, tried to advise and Janey looked bored.

'I must be getting on. I've bought this doll's pram for Mary. It cost seven pounds. I'm telling you. Seven pounds. Come back with me to see it. You're ever so good to me.'

Van rang Miss Birch at the Society of Friends. She arranged to call on Van one afternoon, saying it would be better if Janey wasn't in the house. The Quaker lady was dressed as a man and carried a suitcase. Her face was big and hairy. She wore pebble glasses and her head was cropped. Short back and sides. In a toneless voice she said, 'I'm delighted to meet you. I've been thinking for a long time that one of the Friends should come and have a little chat with you about Janey. We are very worried about her. I expect you know the story?'

Van said 'Yes.'

'Those people down below make life very unpleasant for her you know. The man should be imprisoned but we can't get any evidence.'

'The man?' Van was startled. 'I thought it was the woman. Janey always tells me that the woman is a fiend.'

Miss Birch looked perplexed. 'You realise that it's the man who is responsible for Janey's pregnancy? It was he who attacked her at Christmas and now the wife is busy taking it out on her. She seems to have got the whole street on her side.'

'I thought it was her husband.'

'I suppose Janey told you that. Poor Janey. She is a silly girl. No, I'm afraid our Janey has never had a husband. She's a helpless little thing. An excellent home-maker. Her flat is a joy. She decorated it entirely on her own you know. Apart from that she's never had any idea how to look after herself, though it seems likely that Arthur and Mary have the same father.' Miss Birch gave her a stout hand to shake.

Janey was cheerful the next morning. She had picked up a copy of *Lady Chatterley's Lover* in a junk shop and had brought it along as a present for Van. She pushed it into her hand, grinning and giggling.

'I found it in the junk shop. You know, the junk shop. It's lovely there. You ought to go. He's ever so nice. Bill is. He kept this specially for me. I'm telling you straight. Specially for me. Would you like it? They say it's awful. You know — awful.' She clapped her hands to her mouth.

'Janey,' Van said, 'Miss Birch from the Friends came to see me.'

'Doris came to see you? Doris did? That's awful. You shouldn't have done it. I'm telling you. You're ever so good to me. You and Mr Langford, honest you are. It was decent the way he came round that day when I was rotten. Really decent. That's what Arthur said. But you shouldn't have had Doris round. Silly old bitch, forgive me. She is a silly old bitch, heaven help us. She's good and that. Oh, she's good all right but she is a silly old bitch. I go round to her place at weekends. Honestly she and that Sandra she lives with. They're a funny pair. You know what I mean. "My little pussykins" she calls Sandra. Honest she does. I wouldn't tell you if she didn't. "My little pussykins and Fluffy" that's what she calls her. It's funny. I bet she said some dreadful things. She'd like to own me body and soul Doris would. That's it. Body and soul. She used to be a Probation Officer. Did you know? That's how I met her. Honestly she used to be a Probation Officer, silly old cow.'

'What did you have to do with a Probation Officer?' Van asked gently, hoping for a sensible reply.

'Oh that. That was mean that was. It wasn't my fault. Just a pair of stockings at Woolworths and they caught me the rotters. I had bad luck. Old Kathleen, Paddy's wife, she's always at it and they never get her. She's got some lovely things I'm telling you straight. Really lovely. She's a wonderful mother is Kathleen.'

Janey was now in the seventh month of pregnancy and there was no hiding it any longer. Her stomach was enormous. She still wore her green overall for cleaning, but it was a tight fit. The buttons were strained and the skirt rode up above her knees in front. She looked pathetic with her thin face and decaying teeth.

'It's awful not to have a decent man,' she said. 'I deserve a decent man, really I do. The way I bring up those kids. I bring up Arthur just like my own. He's a lovely kid is Arthur. Better than Mary bless her. That's what Kathleen says, Paddy's wife, she says I bring up Arthur just like my own.'

'But Janey, is Arthur not your son then?'

'Don't you go telling Doris that will you? She'd create. Honestly Doris would. She'd say I wasn't decent and that. I'm not having you tell Doris. It was that rotter I took up with before I left Sligo. She'd left him honestly. I wouldn't say that if it wasn't true. She walked out on him and left him with the kid. I was in hospital then doing the cleaning. You know, doing the wards and that. It was awful the suffering. Poor little mite. He was only five months old, poor little blighter. I'd never do that. I took up with him, Arthur's dad that was. I took up with him and then I fell for Mary. Just my luck poor old Janey. I fall easy all right. I'm sorry for Arthur though. It's all right for Mary. She's got my name, but not Arthur poor little kid. They could take him any day. You know. Just walk in and take him. I couldn't stop them honestly. I couldn't. It's awful and now look at me. I've had enough. That's it. I've had enough. I've had a rotten life and I don't deserve it. I'm decent really.'

'Janey. What about the work? Isn't it too much? Couldn't you do less work?'

'Are you trying to get me out?' Janey was crying and she wiped her eyes with her little stained hand. She wore a thin wedding ring. She had probably bought it at Bill's.

'If only I'd got rid of it when I tried. Earlier on like. I tried everything. I went to that shop down the North End Road. You know, where the market is. There's a shop there Kathleen told me about. That's where Rita got her syringe and it worked for her. They're all against me. It worked for Kathleen and Rita. It's rotten really how it never worked for me. I did my best though I'm telling you. Nobody can say I didn't do my best to ged rid of the poor little bastard. I took pills too. I got a whole box of pills down there. Don't you believe them when they tell you it works. Nothing works. I'm telling you straight, and I should know after all I've been through.'

What resolution Janey showed in the face of her rotters and her pregnancies. She had not had the wherewithal to fall into the good hands of James and Henry. One rotter and Van was annihilated, scuppered into dissolution.

The characters in Janey's tale were queer. Doris and Sandra, Kathleen and Paddy, Mary and Arthur. The North End Road and the Meeting House in Blythe Road, the junk shop and Woolworth's and the neighbours in the sad street by the gasworks.

Janey did as Van suggested and started to come in only twice a week to do some light work. Van didn't bother her with questions. She made her drink a pint of milk at eleven instead of coffee. They didn't talk about the baby.

Van and Martin had planned to take Melissa to the sea for a month at the end of September. Janey's baby was due on the sixteenth or thereabouts. The die was cast and the Quakers were in charge. When they returned Van hoped to find some sign from Janey but was disappointed. Two days after they got home she went in search. She began by going to the flat, imagining that all being well, Janey would have left hospital. The woman from downstairs opened the door.

'They've gone. Them and the bastard too. They've all gone.'

'Are they coming back?'

'How should I know if the whore's coming back? She's left her things. I can tell you that. She's been gone weeks.'

'The postman's been at it again,' thought Van; the woman's stomach was swollen in advanced pregnancy.

She drove to St Stephen's Hospital. There they told her that Janey had had a baby boy some weeks before. She had been very ill and two women had come in a car to take her away. 'Doris and Pussykins of course. I wonder where Mary and Arthur are?' she thought, and went to ring up the Society of Friends. Doris told her that Janey was at a cottage in the country.

'The Friends have several you know. She's well off down there and it's good for Mary and Arthur. Just while she convalesces. When it's all over I'm afraid she'll have to go back to her flat.'

Janey's life was tragic. Her own was not. She must not glorify her misery. Reinforced by their kind-heartedness, Van said goodbye to James and Henry and returned to her empty house. It had to be tucked up for the winter. Spiralling the bend at the top of her drive, she sensed the unexpected. There was company awaiting her: Rupert and Lucy. In the sitting-room a fire flamed. Logs were burning, rightful logs intended for the grate. Her friends had come to make amends. Aware, dimly, of having, simply by the act of their existence, played some part in her defeat, they had driven many miles to show love. Rupert had remembered that her birthday was near and had visited the ironmonger in the village below. He had spotted a new line there in autumn 'gifts'. Huge and heavy, a long-handled pan brimming with chestnuts and covered in cellophane was topped with a pink paper bow. They held it out to her. The base of the pan was punctured with holes. It was ready for use. Stripping it of its trimmings, they leant to the fire; faces reddening, avoiding bad topics. Young and considerate, they helped her to close the house, wrapping the extractable keyboard from the piano in a blanket. Rupert carried this upstairs and set it on a shelf away from damp patches.

With the help of Rupert and Lucy, she packed Johann's books into her car.

Then her friends drove away in convoy: Lucy, pretty as a bunch of grapes, at the wheel of the car borrowed by Johann. There were two new dents in one of the panels. Johann had made a hash of a twist in the road.

James and Henry were right. Absolutely right. She must make a clean break. She mustn't let them down. They had given shelter, comfort, and valuable time. They would become her imaginary audience as she conducted herself with dignity in the months to come. She gathered strength to meet her needs. A thousand miles of road lay ahead of her. The books she would drop at a London club. She would not see him. Ever again.

Firm and weary, she reserved a room for the night at a hotel in France. It was just over the border. She had passed, once again, through the Mont Blanc Tunnel. By rights Johann should have been with her. Alone in the foyer, she ordered a glass of red wine and sat to re-read the poem that had inspired her on her outward trip. No wild nights now. She was lonely and afraid. In bed, clipping at her nails, she compared her lot, once again, with that of Janey.

It had not been until after Christmas that year that Van had seen Janey again. She was driving down the King's Road when she caught sight of her. It was cold and Janey was wearing an old winter overcoat she had given her. She was carrying a parcel and was looking, as usual, at the ground.

Van stopped and called out. 'Janey. How are you? Why didn't you come to see us?'

'I should have honestly. I know I should. Here. Look at this. I bought it in the junk shop. Round at Bill's. It's a water colour. It's genuine. I'm telling you. Do you like it? You can have it. I'd like you to have it honestly. You and Mr Langford. Come on. You have it.'

'Thank you, Janey. I'd like it very much. I'll put it in Melissa's room. It's pretty. Are you still in the flat?'

'That flat. Yes. Isn't it awful? They keep on at me there. That bitch is carrying. Serve her right. She'll see what it's like. Perhaps she'll leave me alone when she's got her own kid, poor little devil. I wouldn't be her kid, honestly. Perhaps she'll leave me alone and stop saying I'm a whore and that. She was awful when I got back. "What have you done with the bastard?" she said. Honestly, isn't that a wicked thing to say to a mother? Arthur'll tell you straight. "What's your Mum done with the bastard?" she said to Arthur. Honestly. I'm telling you.'

Van was delighted to see Janey again. They planned that she would go to the flat with Martin the following evening. Janey was skipping about when they arrived. The flat was fuller than ever with trophies from Bill's shop.

'What do you think of these? Old Janey and the junk shop! Aren't I awful? They're real these candlesticks. That's what Bill said. Real. Ninepence for two. Honestly, only ninepence. It was rotten in the hospital. It's a lousy hole that place. They never should have let me see him. They shouldn't have.

Knowing I have to give him up. I told them. I said they were rotten to do it poor little devil.'

'Poor Janey. Anyway it's over. You have made it nice here. Can we sit down?'

'Yes. Go on. Sit anywhere. How's Melissa? She's a lovely kid. I told Kathleen she's a lovely little kid.'

Van asked where Mary and Arthur were.

'Oh them. They're up there in the attic. They love it up there. It's nice for kids. I'm lucky having this place. They'll be down in a minute the little devils. Mary. She's awful Mary is. She's worse than the boy. They really break your heart honestly.' Van was enjoying herself.

'Tell me more Janey. I rang Miss Birch. She told me you were in the country.'

'It was all right. The country. Ever so lonely though. Really lonely. It was nice for the kids. I'd do anything for the kids. Listen, I went to the theatre yesterday. I'm telling you. Up to the West End. This fellow I met in the pub, Ronald he's called. He gave me two tickets. He works there. That's it. He works in the theatre. I took Rita. She's had a rotten life, Rita has. She's got a rotten husband. She keeps telling me I'm better off without one even if they call me a whore. Poor old Rita.'

Arthur and Mary came into the room. They were in full fancy dress. Van recognised one of her scarves. It was strapped around Mary's chest, used as a bust-bodice. Arthur wore a cowboy outfit and a woman's felt hat. They were convulsed with laughter and Janey looked proudly at them.

'Go on Arthur. Say hello. She won't. Mary won't. Go on Arthur. You say hello. He's a good boy, Arthur is.' Janey, watching her guests, decided to join in. She snatched at a needle-work cushion, doubtless from the junk shop, and pulled it over her head, clasping it under the chin with one hand.

'I'm as bad as the kids. That's where they get it from, poor little blighters. Come on Arthur. Mary, you get in the middle.'

They danced a disorganised jig and then Janey made tea.

'It was good of you to come,' she said. 'I'll tell Kathleen and Rita. I'll tell them straight.'

Janey called a few days after the visit. Van carried coffee through to the drawing-room. Janey was thrilled.

'Aren't I posh? Real posh. Good old Janey. I am awful. What can you think? It looks nice here.' Janey wore a look of territorial suspicion. The gap she had left behind her must, surely, have been filled by now. 'What's she like? Not such a bother as poor old Janey I bet. Poor old Janey with all her worries. Honestly you were good to me.' Van offered her the job back. Janey said, 'Thank you ever so much. I'd like that. There are some rotten jobs.'

'I'm glad, Janey. I was frightened you wouldn't want to come back here after all you went through last year.'

'I did. I had a rotten year. Come on. Let's forget it. That's it. Let's forget all about it. Bastard and all, poor little devil, bless his soul. He's gone to a lovely home. Really decent. He'll have a good time there. Better than I could give him poor kid. That's what Rita said. "You did right Janey." You can ask anyone. That's what she said. Would you like me to start now? Cleaning and that? I can, honestly. I'm fine now. Thanks for the coffee. Was it Nescafé or was it proper? You know, proper? Fancy old Janey drinking proper coffee like that in the drawing-room. Honestly. Cheerio.'

She settled in. Occasionally she would miss a day but always managed to explain it away in her own slippery fashion.

'Did you think I wasn't coming back? You shouldn't think that, honestly. It was this fellow Ronald. The one I met in the pub. He's posh. "My dear Janey," he says. I'm telling you, "My dear Janey". Arthur and Mary think the world of him, but I'm not having anything to do with men. Not men. They're rotten.'

'What did Ronald have to do with your staying away, Janey? My mother came to lunch and I kept putting off doing the house, thinking you'd be coming. It looked a mess.'

'I got this gramophone from Bill. You know. An old one. There was a record on it honestly. He didn't know. Bill didn't. I got it cheap. Seven shillings, with this record on. Ronald said he'd fix it. Yo know. Fix it. He's good, Ronald is, silly beggar.

He said he'd be round at eight. Eight o'clock honestly, before I took the kids to school. I wasn't going to have that bitch downstairs interfering saying I had men in and that. I had to wait in for him. He's a lazy bastard old Ronald. He didn't come round until twelve. They missed school poor little devils. Not Arthur, he's a nice boy Arthur. It's her. She a proper little bitch heaven help her.'

Van said that she was glad Janey had met a decent man, even if he was lazy. She asked Janey to come up and see Melissa.

'She can crawl now but she does it in an odd way with one leg tucked underneath her. It makes her travel sideways like a crab. Did either of yours ever do that?'

'Oh them. Heaven help us. Look at this. It's a letter to the Mayor. The Mayor of Sligo. You know. Where I come from. Ronald wrote it. He's educated and that, Ronald is. There's property there. Old Janey and her mansion. I told Ronald about it. There's this house. It ought to come to me. My mother's gone. Paddy told me. He heard from this other girl. Kathleen's friend. She comes from Sligo. She's gone. My mother's gone. Silly old bitch my mother. She was honestly. She never should have done it. Treated me like that. Look at old Janey speaking ill of the dead. She made me what I am. He was American my father. That's what they say. Honestly. American.'

Van asked what Ronald had said in the letter.

Dear Sirs,

I have reason to believe that my mother, the late Mrs Bashford now deceased, had property in Sligo which should now be mine. I would like all details to be sent to me by return of post.

Your obedient servant.

Janey read it with pride, hands shaking with excitement.

'That's Ronald all over. "Dear Sir." He's posh Ronald is. Educated.'

The tragedy occurred soon after Easter. Van was in a deep sleep when the telephone rang early one morning. It was a Miss

Pettigrew from the Society of Friends.

'Miss Birch asked me to ring you. I'm afraid I have some terrible news. Mary died at the weekend. Janey's daughter, Mary. It was an accident. I don't know the ins and outs I'm afraid, but it seems Janey has been very careless. Something to do with pills that were lying around. Mary found them and died soon after swallowing them. If you ring Miss Birch later she will give you more information. She is with Janey now but will be in the office later in the morning.'

What a wilderness of despair. Drama and tragedy were a part of Janey, but not this. This was too horrible. Van cried, and thoughts of Mary ran through her head. 'Cheeky little bitch. Cheeky little bastard Mary is, I'm telling you.' She banged her head on the pillow. The Quakers were kind. She was grateful to them. 'She's a little monster. I chastise her. She's worse than the boy.'

Van got up and went to Janey's flat. Miss Birch was there drinking tea with Arthur. He looked strained and didn't speak.

'They kept Janey in the hospital,' Miss Birch told her. 'She is very shocked. Meanwhile I will look after Arthur. Come on dear. Try to drink your tea.'

Van wandered into the street. She had been sick before leaving her house and now she felt dizzy. She leant on the railings outside Janey's flat and looked down into the area, into the tumbling jumble of dustbins, egg shells, broken shoes and milk bottles.

Martin went with her to the funeral. It was in the cemetery in the Fulham Road, opposite the hospital where Mary had been taken in the ambulance and where, only a few months before, Janey had given birth to the postman's son. It was a strange party that saw Mary to the grave. Janey wore a long black coat, nearly down to the ground; she and Arthur clung together. Miss Birch was there with 'Pussykins'. Paddy and Kathleen. Rita looked very smart. Ronald came with his mother. She saw Bill from the junk shop. There were some strangers too. The coffin was small. Van thought of a velvet box her mother had once sacrificed to put a baby rabbit in. She watched Janey clinging to Arthur. They were everything to each other and yet no tie of birth or law bound them. Janey came to call shortly afterwards. She was still wearing the long black coat bought from Bill. Bill had given it to her in fact.

'She never should have done it. She'll never learn Mary won't. I kept telling her not to touch them pills. It was them pills I had last year to get rid of the baby. You know. I told you. I got them in the North End Road, I never should have kept them. Poor little Mary. She was a decent kid, honestly. It was them that done it. I wouldn't have had pills if it hadn't been for them. That's it. They're murderers. I had to chastise her. She was dreadful. Mary was. She died in my arms. "Hold me Mum," she said. It was dreadful. She kept saying it, "Hold me Mum." Them downstairs. They killed Mary.'

Van took Janey into the drawing-room and lit the fire. She was shivering.

'The priest came round. You know. Catholic. He was good to me. They are decent, Catholics. They can be decent. He sat with me while Mary died. The ambulance was too late. She'd gone by the time they arrived. He came with me in the ambulance and that. Kathleen got him round. Kathleen from next door. He was decent.'

After the inquest Janey and Arthur moved to the country. The Friends decided that she couldn't continue in the flat and they returned her to one of their cottages. She was made responsible for cleaning the Meeting Room down there. Arthur went to the village school.

Van sent Janey a hundred cigarettes for Christmas and a toy dart board for Arthur. She read Janey's letter of thanks aloud to Martin.

'Thanks for our nice presents. It was decent of you to remember us. I am pleased to hear that you have another little girl. Melissa must be pleased too as she is of an age to take notice. I do miss you all honestly. I did love working for you. Arthur and I would like to come and see you whenever suitable as I know how busy you must be. I have some news I know you will be pleased to hear. I am getting married some time in the

New Year to a very nice fellow. Doris has met him and she thinks he's a very nice fellow. I will let you know the date. Perhaps you could all come down for the day.'

Janey had had courage in spite of rotters.

The past didn't help. Neither Van's own nor that of others.

At Dover she forgot her imaginary audience. James and Henry had faded into the distance. She was back in Johann's world. He was only a telephone call and an hour and a half by road away. A telephone call couldn't hurt. She would use the books in her car as an excuse. She rang his number.

'Wonderful woman,' he said. 'I will cook you something special. Birthday lunch.'

It was her birthday and a lump, to which she had become accustomed, was lodged in her throat.

Looking chipper, he opened the door and planted a noisy kiss on her lips. She had started her journey in Arras that morning and had crossed the channel, had driven from Dover to Kennington and was tired out. It had become the pattern of her life. The kitchen was in disarray and the chef was wearing a butcher's apron. A great deal of preparation was in progress. Terrine or some such thing. She could not concentrate on food talk. On the table beside the terrine was an envelope with her name written on it. Inside there was a birthday card, but not only that. Folded into the card there was a small square ticket, stiff and cardboardy. She was, for a year, a member of the London Library. Her 'massive interlect' had always awed him. She yearned for headscarves and scent, furs and chocolates from her lover. Here was a final rejection and a very generous one. A sort of pay-off. Thanking him gently, she tried to eat. The terrine was greasy and made her feel slightly faint. This might be her last chance. Were he to relent, she would succumb. Back at square one. After the fiasco of the last escapade, there she was, in his house, having lugged his books across Europe, prepared to forgive him. She clung to him as she left, praying for a reprieve. Would he, after all, take her upstairs, settle her under the duvet, and ask her to squeeze him like a toothpaste tube? The Dettol remained on her Tuscan dressing table.

He dismissed her, promising to telephone in the evening.

'We will meet in the London Library. I shall show you around. I became a member myself last year. It is useful to me in my work. We will lunch together.'

That was to be it. Light lunches and dark hunts in library passages. Overnight she was to become a maiden aunt; amusing and well educated. His nights were reserved for fleeting fancies. After her initiation as a reading member followed by a light lunch, he told her that he had been offered the use of a house, a large one, not far from where she lived. Twenty miles away. It couldn't be possible. The offer appealed to him and he had decided to take it up for a few weeks. They would, he told her, meet frequently for lunch. 'Best friends in the world.'

Something happened on her domestic front which had a bearing, albeit remote, on the path of deterioration along which she was travelling. Polly had recently acquired a pony. Miranda, she was called. She grazed in a field opposite the house amongst black and white cows and one elderly male donkey. The donkey, Neddy, had belonged to Van's mother and had been sent in a horse-box, many years back, as a present to the granddaughters. Even then nobody knew his age or the limits of his sexual capacities. Now he had been joined by Polly's young mare.

Neddy was a well-loved character in the village, waking the population as he often did, in the early hours with a rasping bray, lasting sometimes for many minutes at a stretch. Van's neighbour said that it reminded him of Italy during the war. Nobody complained.

After the arrival of Miranda it began to cross Van's mind that they might be landed with a mule. Nobody knew whether or not Neddy had ever been gelded. The vet was sent for to offer his opinion. He came, a young and swarthy gypsy. Together they crossed the road, carrots and halters in hand, to investigate. Van clung to the donkey, her arms around his neck and her face buried in his thick dusty coat whilst the vet groped for male organs. She thought of Johann and of James's suggestion that she should have cut his balls off with a carving knife. Perhaps that would happen to Neddy. Perhaps her son would have been some sort of a mule.

'He's all male, poor old fellow,' the vet told her. 'But he's too old to operate on. You're running a risk, leaving him here with your daughter's pony. Ever so sorry, but you really ought to have him put away. He's pretty rickety – I doubt he'd last much more than another winter in any case.'

She stared, forlornly, at Neddy, remembering Johann's broken down look when, with James and Henry, she had gone to send him packing.

The alternatives, the vet told her after she had paid him ten pounds for the visit, were these. A delegation from the vet's surgery could come and shoot him in the field. She would have to bury him herself. How on earth could she bury a donkey? And then there would be the shot, with half the village out to witness the murder of their pet. Safari in their midst.

'The alternative?' she asked.

'Ring up the kennels. That would be the easiest. They'll come round with a humane killer and they'll remove the carcass. Feed it to the hounds. I should do that if I were you.'

A man with a lisp answered when she rang the kennels. They made an appointment to meet at the gate of the field at ten o'clock the following day. By then the school children would have passed by and be trapped in the classroom. A truck and trailer with a canvas covering drove up as the clock struck ten. Out jumped a man wearing a cloth cap pulled down over his face; his collar was turned up. Very thin, he was, and she fancied him to be masked, as a burglar in a children's book.

He walked, as did Johann, silently on the balls of his feet. Some sort of apparatus protruded from his jacket and a grin was fixed to his lips.

Van caught the donkey, patted him, feeding him an apple. Then, faint with fear, she handed the halter to her companion who had tip-toed up beside her. He struggled to attach the apparatus to Neddy's head, a sort of band – like ear-phones – in so far as she could bear to look.

She turned away. A ping went through her head and she was sick. When she turned back Neddy was still standing, but beginning to rock. His head drooped as his neck weakened. Slowly his four legs spread outwards in defeat. He behaved like a wooden toy controlled from within by elastic strands. Then his head flopped and blood trickled from between his long teeth. He fell, heavy as lead, as Johann had done at the bottom of her stairway. Her accomplice turned to fetch the trailer. She did not watch as Neddy's body was hauled, a collared rope around him, on to the truck. The canvas sheet was secured to cover his body and the driver made as to leave. Now Van was efficient, in charge. She thanked him politely.

'Sad,' she said, 'but, since it had to be done, you couldn't have made it easier. It really is a humane killer.'

'Yeth,' he answered, looking sly from under his cap. 'It's ever so easy' (lisping the while). 'That's how my Mum done herself in last Christmas.'

'Good God,' she said. 'Why?'

'Trouble with a fellow.'

He touched his cap and drove off. A day or two later, Van saw the hounds and bit her lip. It was easy to kill; horrifying that she should have had the power to exterminate poor Neddy. The hounds, the image of her pyre and the image of her mule-like son battered at her brain. Sometimes her son would be in the flames and sometimes he would be a donkey, wearing an ass's head. She read and re-read *A Midsummer Night's Dream* and listened, often more than once at a sitting, to Verdi's *Trovatore* on the gramophone. In the opera Azucena, the gypsy had hurled her own son into the flames of a fire. She, poor woman, had been bereft of her senses.

Winnie lived in a caravan with seven cats at the bottom of the garden, across the stream, on the site of an abandoned tennis court. Strangers were accustomed to wonder why she was not a man. Martin's mother, Babs, had met her at a cat show. Babs, a rally driver of high acclaim, was responsible for the entry into England of the first BMW. Van and Martin had inherited eleven vintage cars, the house, the garden, some cats and Winnie.

Shoulders bent forward, Winnie cornered Van in the courtyard. She had strictures to issue. Vanessa was neglecting her inheritance.

'There's been more going on than what you know of. And what happened to the weed-killer? Sodium chlorate for the paths? I've left you a dozen notes.'

Half of Van's mind was absent. That day she had written to Johann. It was a catastrophe. She was without pride. Her words had become foul. Foul fiends.

'Now I know,' she wrote, 'I had too much love in me. I was an orange that you squeezed dry. You kept the skin, the outer casement, having swallowed what was good within. You stuck cloves into it, thinking it might come in handy one day for airing your linen. Now I am leathery and shrivelled, pierced in every pore. That is my conclusion.' It was posted and Van tried to extract the letter from the box.

Muriel Bush, passing on her way to take her turn at the village shop, a community venture kept afloat by voluntary help from the ladies of Rockingbourne, saw Van battling to withdraw the letter.

'Once posted, letters are the property of the GPO. It doesn't seem fair does it? Something you regret?' She whipped out her diary. When could Van take her turn to serve in the shop?

Van had always enjoyed serving in the shop. She had written a jingle; a contribution to a fund-raising enterprise.

'You start at the bottom and rise to the top
At the Rockingbourne Venture Community Shop.
Of intoxicant liquor they sell not a drop
At the Rockingbourne Venture Community Shop.'

It had continued in this style, incorporating names of village characters. The shop was missing her.

Dressed, always, as a man, a recently acquired earth closet in a shed her pride and joy, Winnie groaned and grumbled; terrorising the village children, knocking heads together were their owners to so much as steal a plum. At first she had scared the living daylights out of Van; the figure in hob-nailed boots, an abomination at the bottom of her garden. Babs said 'You'll take to Winnie. She's honest and she'll chase any burglar off. Be good to her. Invite her to lunch on Christmas day and take her to the town once a week to shop. She has a motor bike but she can't carry cat food on that. Take her on a Friday.'

They had become a well-known pair. Winnie, wearing collar and tie, collecting her copy of *Fur and Feather* on weekly order at the newsagent; Van, attentive, driving cautiously for fear of reprimand.

These absorbtions took second place, her letter sitting there in the box; the property of the GPO.

She looked out, through the arched window of her kitchen, past a knotted walnut tree, to the garden. Polly was away and Miranda grazed, neglected, fattening in the field. She should have been allowed her mule. They both should. Lance, the garden boy, had lit a bonfire and the smoke was heading for Winnie's washing line. She would be bound to grumble. How could it matter? On the line hung dungarees and a man's shirt; not frilly smalls or cami-knickers.

Van met Johann for lunch in a market town near where she lived and near where he was residing in state in the mansion he had been lent.

He had grown a moustache. Barely more, in its early stages, than a shadow above his lip, it occurred to her in her state of highly-wrought expectation that it was a cry for help. He was hiding from her and her fantasies.

'I wondered when you were going to notice it.' He was not flirtatious now, but quiet and sad.

'Can I visit you in your palace, Johann?'

'You're potty,' he said. 'Completely potty. After that letter you wrote me.' Stroking his moustache across the table, she asked him what he was escaping from.

'This and that,' he told her. He called to a waitress and asked her to bring him a glass of water. 'I'm living the life of a monk. My script is going badly. You have driven me from Italy. Don't drive me, now, from my last retreat.'

Speaking fast, she told him of the murder in her field. He looked terrified.

'Don't Van. Please don't. You scare me. Frightening woman. You might slip a halter round my neck.' He had to go to the lavatory.

The waitress came and stood beside her. 'Your husband asked for a glass of water.' Entirely contented, Van thanked the girl and drank the water.

'That bloody woman hasn't brought me my water,' he grumbled, sitting down.

'She's not bloody. She thought you were my husband.' Now she had nothing to lose. 'I wish you were. I drank it. Ask her for more. I want her to think it again.' There was a warmth between them. They might still have been lovers. The hair above his lip caused havoc inside her as he kissed her in the market square, promising that she could visit him before long in his new abode.

'When I have come to a halt in my writing,' he said. He told her that he loved her still and that he would summon her in a day or two.

The black images faded as she ironed and stitched at her clothing in preparation for their next meeting. When he loved her she had no fears. In the town she bought a pair of shoes. They were bright red, patent leather, with high heels and jaunty buckles. Only whores wear red shoes, Uncle Jim had told her. It was a well-known fact. The last pair she had had, the ones she had worn when she kicked Johann on the shin outside her house in Italy two summers before, on their first official meeting, were worn out. Once, when she was wearing them, her Uncle had said, 'I like your whore's shoes, darling.' She thought he had said 'horse-shoes' and had, since, from time to time, expected to see Miranda canter up, red shoes encircling her hoofs.

On the morning of the day, the magic day, when she was to go to him for the evening, perhaps for the night, he rang her up.

'Beautiful woman. Can you bring me some vegetables? It's starvation corner here. Any vegetables. How does one make a bortsch? Any vegetables and a decent brown loaf.'

The clock had turned back, as she had dreamed it would. She was in the garden, bottom in the air, tugging at the last of the carrots.

In her red shoes, she rounded a curve and drove through an archway into a large cobbled courtyard. He had told her to drive to the back of the house. The front door was not in use. The housekeeper was cantankerous, and Johann was trying to keep signs of his occupation there down to the minimum.

Ice-cold champagne was brought out and the cork, when released from the bottle, hit the wall, ricocheted, and caught Van sharply in the leg. It happened at great speed and the impact, although the pain was not severe, produced a yellow bruise later in the week.

Johann went to attack the vegetables, telling her to look around. Champagne glass in hand, Van made a tour. The house belonged to a wandering Greek. A spirited scribbler, an international yacht-owning millionaire, a health-freak and a seducer of beautiful women. Now he was away for a spell but, when in residence, was renowned for throwing wild and lavish house parties. She wondered how Johann had come to know him.

In the hall, the one through which she had been forbidden to enter, there was a long refectory table. On it lay a black leather book. 'Visitors' was engraved upon it in gold letters. Leafing through, her eye was caught. Last August. The second week. Two names. Johann and Carola. His signature, wiggly and foreign, above hers, feminine and flowery. Van knew it well. 'Massive interlect' in that very hand was engraved upon her mind's eye. That must have been after their trip to Northumberland. They had probably come straight here and spent some days with the Greek. Perhaps he was a friend of Carola's.

It never ended.

Viciously, she scrubbed at the names with lipstick, rendering them unreadable, scarring the page.

Johann was whistling, crushing herbs and treading lightly.

'Why didn't you tell me?' she shouted at him, swiping the garlic crusher from his hand. 'You were here with Carola in August. You told me about Northumberland and you said that was all. I could have heard from someone else. The house was full. I've seen the guest list. They all signed their names. Why did you hide the truth from me?'

'Oh Van,' he said wearily. 'I hoped you would never find out. At any rate not for a year or two. I knew it was fatal to let you come here. I'd forgotten about the book. Grass is green and women are difficult. Have some soup.'

'Where else did you go together? Where did you take her?'

'All right. I took her to the Pathfinders. You know. That couple I've mentioned to you. That's all. Now you know everything.'

'When was that?'

'Last June.'

'Last June? When I was ill?' She remembered now. It was when she was lying, bleeding, racked with pain, on the floor beside the Aga cooker trying to keep warm after her return from the clinic. He had told her he was staying with people called Pathfinder that weekend. She remembered because it was a queer name. No mention had been made of taking a companion with him.

'I've scarred your names with lipstick.'

There was a flash of anger in his hard black eyes.

'Christ Almighty woman! You are mad. That's final. You should go to a shrink. It'd take a genius to sort you out. Here I am, living in someone else's house and you think fit to come and deface the property.'

There they went again. It was as if he wanted things to go wrong. Why had he signed his name in the book? It is easy to dodge that sort of thing, at the last moment, when people are leaving, doors opening and shutting. He allowed her to stay the night. No duvets here. Linen sheets and soft square pillows. He held her tightly in his arms and told her that he loved her but that they must have no more rows. He asked her to rub the back of his neck. She took off her wedding ring. She had never done that before and she hid it, guiltily, behind a book. The curious thing was that, in the morning, she could not find it. She was never able to wear it again.

'Please Johann. Please take me to visit the Pathfinders. I know you can't take me to Northumberland. That was her beat. I'm here now. I've stayed here.' She prayed that they were not occupying the bed that he had shared with Carola in August.

'Give me, at least, what you gave her.'

'Do you want a headscarf? That's all I ever gave her. I did buy her some scent once but that . . . Hem, hem.'

'Of course not. I want to meet your friends. You've met mine. Look at Rupert and Lucy. It's not fair.'

'Very well, but you won't take to them and they won't like you much either. That's why I never offered to take you before. You're so different, Van, to the other people I know. Wait and see.'

That day she rode Miranda. Polly had extracted a promise from her mother that the pony would be exercised while she was away at boarding school. Van, in a mental waste land, swerving, by the hour, from a state of inertia to one of violent energy, was not honouring her commitment. She must take herself in hand. Viewed from the saddle, the ground was a mile away. It was as if she was at the top of a tilting skyscraper. She thought back to the rain and the flyover at Genoa. She thought of Uncle Jim and wished that she didn't have to neglect him. He would be saddened by her continued state of war with Johann. He would advise her, kindly, to give in; call it off. She would not be able to take his advice. For the present she must do without him. She thought of James and Henry and their determination to rescue her from the 'monster'. Nothing and nobody could.

Over a hedge and far off, in a field, she saw two beasts on their hind legs, performing a dance. They looked, although it was difficult to tell at that distance, like monkeys. It was a hornpipe or a Scottish reel. The Gay Gordons perhaps. They fell on all fours and ran behind each other, fast forming a tight circle. Two hares engaged in a love duet. She thought of Johann and the excruciating grip in which he held her.

The fishmonger in Marketborough had a high reputation; a family concern, it belonged to and was run by father, mother and son. The son, nineteen years old, had embarked on a moustache; so many moustaches. At first, not worthily under way, it showed promise and covered only a little of his face. He was a sweet boy, gentle and helpful, and kept the marble slabs fresh and clean. 'Off shore fish' they concentrated on, nonetheless selling all species; roe, soft or hard, salmon, pink and shiny. Van had filled in a form. It had been sent to her by a 'good guide' editor in search of top quality food shops all over the country. After many months of waiting 'Hyslop and Son' were ennobled. Listed, now, in a National Series, sporting a badge in the window. Higher than a knighthood. Van was given special treatment. Trays of eggs and fishy parcels were carried by the boy to her car.

Polly had developed a craving for smoked chicken. She had eaten it somewhere, at a picnic with school friends, and Van felt it a possibility that 'Hyslop and Son' might have a smokery hidden away on their premises. They sold smoked trout, haddock and salmon. Perhaps they had the wherewithal to perform the rite themselves.

'By the way,' she said gently to the boy one morning after he had accompanied her, packets in hand, to the car. 'Do you smoke chicken?'

Pulverised, shell-shocked, he answered 'Never in the shop.'

'Do you do it anywhere else?'

'Sometimes.' Panic stricken.

'Would you ever do it for me?'

'I don't know what you mean.'

'Well. Just occasionally perhaps. Would you do it for me as a special favour if you don't like to do it for everybody?'

The boy feared that she had softening of the brain and had been overtaken by a kinky desire to watch him smoke a cigarette. Funny to address him as 'chicken'.

It was only later that Van understood the nature of the misunderstanding. Now she couldn't return there. She was losing her grip in every direction.

Janet Pathfinder was an overblown thing and her husband a near half-wit, Van thought as they sat in the flowerless drawing-room of an immensely large, incongruous bungalow; verandah-trimmed as a reminder of the Veldt, before dining. Surfaces shimmered with trendy toys. Mervyn, the host, a man of millions from South Africa, sloshed wine into glasses designed for giants. His ginger-white hair was smarmed down, parted with a ruler; his general appearance sleek and sallow. He looked randily at Van, sizing her up for bedworthiness.

'He can't pronounce his r's,' she thought. Janet, his fourth wife, was the daughter of an earl. Lady Janet. She looked hot; hot and hairy in a fluffy red frock, tier upon tier, her neck constricted with pearls. Her bosoms were enormous, pinched and bursting. Black hair, possibly tinted, brushed into a bee-hive, was firm set. Her predecessor had been pensioned off after a car crash had robbed her of her wits.

'People to meet you.' Mervyn's speech was laconic. The 'people' shortly to arrive were show guests.

'They're good news. The Sheltons. Do you know them? Racing buffs.'

Janet looked at Van; Johann's ageing piece. Van looked back at her and thought of the rhinos she had visited with Uncle Jim on the day Johann had first telephoned from Hamburg. Johann bit his nails and picked his nose. Van mourned the wedding ring she had lost in Johann's bedroom.

'You look both common and homosexual with that moustache,' Janet remarked. 'What does Carola think of it?'

'Now, now. No bitchery.' Mr Pathfinder was on the way to the front door.

The star guests entered the room, hot-foot from the races. Strung around with binoculars and trailed by Greta, his mousy wife, Wallace Shelton spat as he shouted about armpits and deodorants. Janet nearly split her sides.

A little girl in a dirty nightdress slithered up to her mother, breath coming in sobs; her face smudgy with tears. Nobody paid her any attention. At dinner Mervyn decanted bottle after bottle. The table was round and conventionally set with silver and damask. Van, drunk, couldn't eat and shouted across the racing buff to Lady Janet.

'What did you think of Carola when Johann brought her here last June? That was when I was ill.'

'For Christ's sake' – Johann, soup on his hairy upper lip. 'Behave yourself.'

The little girl, still tearful, stood beside him. She asked Johann why he had grown a moustache. 'You didn't have one before. Not when you came with that other lady.'

Janet said, 'Carola? Oh we love her. She's bliss, but then Johann nearly always brings stunning women here. We're fussy you know.'

'So, what got into you?' asked Janet as the three women closed in together in the sitting-room. The men stayed behind, drinking more.

'I'm in love with Johann. That's all.' Van wiped away tears from her eyes and chain smoked. Mrs Shelton, kind and fastidious, leant forward. 'Don't dear. You're a bit drunk. You'll be OK. You mustn't be in love with him. He doesn't know how to behave.'

'Greta. How dare you? He's one of our oldest friends. Mervyn knew him when he first came to England in the early days, before he married Myra. Mervyn hadn't lived here long himself. I agree, though, Johann doesn't and never will know how to behave. The way he sat there picking his nose.'

They were joined by the small band of men, now terribly intoxicated. Wallace came over to where Van sat, weeping and lonely. He squeezed and kissed her with exaggerated passion. In her drunken state she rejoiced. To be kissed like that in front of Johann. Greta, dainty, did her best to distract the others but had no luck with Mervyn. His eyes bulged as he queued for his fun. Soon it came. He wrenched her from Wallace's arms, a rag doll, lifted her skirt and felt about inside her knickers. Johann was inert but Janet's tiny black eyes were upon them.

'Now,' she said, pushing all guests towards the door, 'I want you to leave. I want to go to bed with my husband. When you have excited him sufficiently' – this to Van 'he will come to bed with me. Get out the lot of you. And Johann, another time bring Carola.'

Van had boshed it. Blown it. This was what she had asked for, to meet his friends and be included in his life. The flames danced again before her eyes and she left her safety belt undone. They went to Johann's bedroom in the house of the Greek, Johann having driven, grim-faced and drunk, along twenty miles of country lanes. Van screamed that Carola was evil. An evil spell had been cast upon him. Thin as a rat, too – she probably had anorexia. She looked like a horse, an anorexic horse, kicking out with glistening red shoes. Van was confused. Even shoes had become a crimson jangle in her mind. 'Did you take her to the Hungry Horse?'

'Very funny.' He would not, probably could not, make love to her that night. He repeated the resolve he had made to her in Italy the day after the destruction of his clothes.

'That's it Van. Never again.' She lunged down into the bed and tugged at a clump of pubic hair growing thick and curly, not speckled black as the hair on his head, but rusty brown like his moustache. His hand, the one that had explored the inside of his nose at the Pathfinders' dinner party, rushed to defend the area under attack. Twisting her fingers, he took control. She had had time to extricate a small cluster but now her finger was damaged. The fourth finger on her right hand. The pain was sharp, later a deadening ache.

The night was awful. In the morning, when she knew it was over, irrevocably and blankly over, she left, weary and overwrought, in her green car and her new red shoes. At home she drank a bottle of ginger wine. That was all she could find. She slept, empty with fear for her future, the hurt finger her only trophy. With Johann it had been hollow, incomplete. He could not love, could not behave like a normal human being, could not be anything but cruel. She had accepted these factors, believing he would love her. In a frantic way she had been happy. Now it was over.

In the night she hardened her heart. He must no longer affect it. Channels in her mind would have to close. Stepping out of bed into furry slippers, she turned on the light and walked with fortitude down the passage to a bulging book-shelf. Hardbacks of different heights were jammed together phosphorescent and colourful. She plucked one out. It had an orange cover and the lettering engraved on it was gold. It would carry her away and defeat her obsession. Shivering, she took it to bed. When she opened it the pages were blank, every one of them. Then she heard the baby cry, a sad sound coming from a wicker basket at the foot of her bed. Again she slipped her feet into the furry slippers and made for the crib. As her hand came down, gently, on the cover, the baby's head began to swell like a flimsy bubble. It grew larger and larger, a football and then a pumpkin, transparent and fluid as oil on a puddle. She clasped it and then the bubble burst, Nothing was left. Now she was hallucinating and panicky. In the morning she was scared, above all of pouring out, either from a kettle or a teapot. The boiling flow could stream for ever. She might pour without stopping, overbrimming the cup and then the saucer; flood the room. Once her mother had described a niece as an 'exposed nerve'. She, too, had become one.

Her mother visited her during this hazy time. She left the whippets in the car, remembering Van's fear of dogs. No-thing was discussed. Van was dedicated to sparing her mother anxiety. The older woman spoke fast, excited by the garden, sad that Van neglected it. She wanted to dig up a clump of king-cups, Marsh Marigolds she called them, from the bank of the stream where Johann had stolen primroses. They would be transplanted – 'uplooted' was her mother's expression for gardening thefts – and grafted into the gloomy verge of her own pond, some miles away.

Together they walked, spades tucked under their arms, down the path, skirted by herbaceous plants, towards the stream. There were scuttles in the long grass, and her mother said 'It's complete tripe, total one hundred per cent trash about rabbits. They loathe borders . . . '

Van remembered a baby rabbit. It had died before being named. She loved all animals, except dogs, afraid of their caninity. Her mother's friend had driven to the house one day carrying a basket covered in a clean linen cloth. The baby rabbit inside was weak and had been found in a corner of the greenhouse beside a crate of beetroot preserved in peat. Van, aged seven, accepted the responsibility of adoption without query.

She made a bed of straw inside a box and dripped milk, a globule from her fingers, into the criss-cross of the clenched mouth. The feeble creature lay in its cradle beside the Aga cooker, a confessional in the kitchen, soaking up the warmth and listening to music softly played on the wireless.

Her mother's brains masterminded all she did – shelling peas, feeding hens, playing the piano and reading to her at night. They never had a rest. They even controlled her appearance. This could have been unnerving, but that she smelt wonderful.

Van didn't care for some of her mother's friends. The women were fine but one or two of the men, particularly the bachelors, gave her the creeps. There was an elderly bachelor staying in the house when the rabbit arrived. Francis Story. He had a large frame and wore dirty clothes; thick socks in shapeless shoes. A thinker of bigoted frivolity, a lascivious homosexual, a contemner, corrupter maybe, of youth, Francis Story was a provocation in the house. He monopolised her mother, following her into the kitchen, glass in hand, wagging his finger to make an incomprehensible point. The cook was away and her mother was doing her best. Lowering his spectacles he would peer over them, wild eyes roving, to gauge the impression he made. From his giant head sprang a cow-lick

– 127 –

lock of hair. His nose spread untidily and his mouth was cavernous and glinting. His chin, the worst bit, jutting and cleft.

This day, in the kitchen, he advanced on the rabbit, dropping cigar ash and holding his hand up to signal that the music should be turned off. Van went to her mother who bent down and whispered, kissing her.

'Don't pay any attention. He's a silly old geezer.'

If anything could save the rabbit it was music. She turned the volume up, very loud. Francis then betrayed fermenting malignity in his expression. Rampant irritation exploded into words, addressed to her mother.

'You should box her ears. I signalled for that perfectly dreadful noise to be subdued and what does she do? Turns it up.'

The child ran down the passage and up some steps to a larder jammed with pickled eggs and hams, mouldy like rainbows, smelling cold and stale. She could hear them talking.

Her mother said, 'She's only seven. Stay in the library. I thought you wanted to work. Why do you have to lurch about after us? Plug it, can't you.'

Mutters, small danger signals, could be heard as he returned to the library. Together Van and her mother turned the volume up and cossetted the creature, breathing still but barely moving. She was alone in the kitchen when the hind legs stiffened. It was afternoon. Two twigs, hitherto flexible, able to change position, were rigid. She turned the blast of music up, twisting the knob.

Johann's fingers.

Kissing the living thing, fingering the weakling, light of touch, she flopped her dark hair over its form and rippled her lips in the fur. Life was ending. She picked the rabbit and its surround of straw from the box and gathered the bundle close. Where was her mother? The library was likely. Along the passage and up flights of low steps, she hugged the rigid-legged pet. Her heart was in rapid motion. They were talking in the library. She slackened pace before entering. Shelves were built out into the room at right angles creating extra book space. Busts of composers and Chinese landscapes, influenced in style by European priests, topped and lined the gaps. Samarkand rugs stretched over the floor, pink and faded, rather tatty. Francis Story was in front of the fire, telling an oft-told tale. She, Van's mother, sat on a comfortable sofa, haloed in hair. The halo was stiff but haphazard, a series of golden roly-polys, each one individually formed and pinned by thin blond hairpins. 'Invisible hairpins', it said on the packet. Her nose was enormous and her eyes were blue as vincas.

There was safety on the sofa. Gathering speed, Van reached the knees and tipped herself onto her mother's body, clasping the rabbit, wetness dribbling from the straw. Settled on the coarse skirt, too thick for the time of year, she clasped her mother, always inappropriately dressed, and the rabbit, now dead.

Words, constrained by the intonation of which Francis Story was so proud, spattered from the club-fender. 'Of course I believe in hypocrisy. What do you think carpets are for? They are there in order to have things swept under them.'

Recent attacks on hypocrisy, made in the press, were among his demonic bugbears. Amongst the many thorns in his flesh. He stopped. He had lost his audience. Van cried into the straw bundle, her mother's arms around her. He advanced a pace towards them.

'Will you be quiet? I was telling your mother a story.'

Together they cringed, and the older one whispered. 'It couldn't be worse. Of course it couldn't. There's a velvet box we can lie him in.'

'Do you want to hear the end of my story?'

Safe in her mother's arms, Van mumbled 'Go away.'

He came nearer, his frame uncontrolled and his face buckled, contorted with temper. 'Will you shut up?'

'Shut up yourself.'

Then he hit out. A large-scale hand shot from a frayed sleeve, meaty and hard. It came down on the leg, looped over her mother's knee. She flinched and let loose a moan. He did it again, then again, harder with each stroke. All three were aghast; Van terror-crazed, her mother pale as ashes, Francis Story feeble and hushed. The bundle of straw fell from the four knotted knees and the contents, a piece of fur, grey and unyielding, bounced onto the Samarkand rug. They were standing and Francis Story came forward. He fished in his pocket, produced a pound note.

'Vanessa,' he said, holding the note out to her, 'buy yourself another rabbit.' Stooping towards the corpse, puce-faced, she muttered, between clenched teeth, 'Go away.'

Now he was practically on all fours, slavering and obsequious.

'I'm going away. You won't have to see me for some time. Forgive me, please, before I go.'

'After that,' her mother said, 'it will have to be at least a year. Vanessa is completely and totally right.' Then, bending over her child, beads swinging, she said: 'There, my darling. There are good Stories and there are bad Stories; sooner or later they all come to an end.'

Now Van wondered, as she looked at her mother in the garden, whether Francis Story had been her lover. His homosexuality had been made much of but one never knew. She thought of Melissa and Polly and of their tormenting hatred of Johann. Would this story ever come to an end?

She could barely manage the mechanical movements of life. There were things to be seen to. Every time Van opened a cupboard door she closed it again with great promptitude. Jam jars were stuck to shelves in the kitchen and mould lined the bread bin. The linen cupboard was the biggest bogey. At one time this had been Van's pride and pleasure. Slatted shelves had been arranged with finicality, catering for every classification. There were labels in her handwriting attached to the various compartments. Large sheets, single sheets, sheets to be mended. Then, below, hand towels, face towels, bath towels and bathing towels; top pillow-cases, under pillow-cases and baby pillow-cases. Now it was a shambles, and every knowing label was betrayed.

She sat down at her desk. She would write to Uncle Jim. There was a clean orange rubber at the end of the pencil she picked up. When she began to write it was as though she was writing with a biro point, not with lead. Fear crept through her.

Was Johann inveterately cruel?

On the side of the pencil, Van noticed of a sudden, letters were stamped as if to show a trade mark. They read: 'This is not a pencil.' It was a joke; a gimmick, a biro built to look like a pencil. Was everything in the house going to cause her to jump out of her skin, her heart to burst her bosom?

Two days after her mother's visit, still in terrible pain, weak and shaken, she rang Uncle Jim. She hadn't succeeded in writing a letter.

'About time too,' he sounded cheerful. 'I'll take the afternoon off. I'll be with you in a couple of hours.'

That evening he took her to the surgery where her finger was inspected. It was swollen and misshapen but not, the doctor thought, broken. An X-ray would have to be taken all the same. In spite of Uncle Jim and his support, the flames increased and the finger, now in a black leather holster, was always a reminder of the lost wedding ring, the drunkenness and the murdered son.

# Chapter
## VII

Vanessa went more often to the local market town. There was always something she needed. Coffee, cigarettes and ginger wine. In the town there was a sandwich bar. Van would insist on a teenage girl buttering rolls and filling them with ham and beef, glued together with mustard. She could tear at them with her teeth in the car, nothing to show for the expedition but crumbs on her frock as she entered the front gate.

In the window of the cleaner's shop there was a sign, scrawled on a child's blackboard, which said 'Duvets cleaned. Your's can be as good as new.' Her stomach contracted. Inside she waited. In front of her in the queue stood an elderly woman, very upright. Her appearance was distinctive. She was tall and her hair grew, grey and thin, starting high above the forehead. Fussily she conferred with the lady behind the counter. Clothes were important to her and the ones she wore expensive; a blue suede jacket lined with fur and a box-pleated tweed skirt. Van ran to the bank and was taken aback to find the same lady in front of her, cashing a cheque. How nippy she must be. Then, at the chemist where Van bought caffeine pills, the same lady there again. In front of her. It was incomprehensible. She couldn't be less than seventy and Van travelled at a great pace. She was scared when she found her in the sandwich bar and smiled, pining for a chat. No smile of recognition was returned. How horrid of her. Watching her down the street for signs of a springy step, Van noticed that she was lame and moved slowly. She, Vanessa, must be nearly mad. After that they passed each other continually in the street and in the shops. To begin with the lady would return Van's smile infrequently; later on each occasion. Sometimes she walked with a limp but often not, altering within the space of minutes. Her mind was slipping. On a day out from school Melissa, spreading healing balm, announced that elderly identical twins had come to the neighbourhood.

A day or two later a long letter came from Melissa. Van sat down to read it, afraid of finding something odd or unwelcome on the pages.

My darling darling Mum

Thanks for the book and those buttons. Nobody plays canasta any more so don't bother about sending cards.

Now Mum. I hope you're not going to mind this. Matron came in last night and said she was anxious about Polly so I rushed over to her house and sat with her in that horrid room by the sick-bay for a bit. She's in a stew about Christmas and the holidays and things and says you don't love us properly any more. I told her that you hadn't been very well and that it was nothing to do with us. Well, anyway, here goes.

It's Johann Kraesel really. He gives her the creeps, and she thinks that he's mucking everything up. I think it's a bit because your letters have got so short. Sort of as if you had to write but don't want to say what's going on. Could you explain to us a bit? What's happened to Uncle Jim anyway? You haven't told us anything about going to plays or Gordon or Miranda or anything for ages. Please don't be cross Mum. We do try to understand but it would be better if he doesn't come down in the holidays. Some girls have been rusticated for drinking in the orchard. Vivien Hagar came reeling into supper and matron smelt her breath. Don't worry. We never get caught. Piles of love. Melissa.

Van answered the letter saying that she loved them, that Johann would not return to either of their houses and that things would improve.

One morning, as a bolt from the blue, Van answered the telephone. It was Michael. Carola's husband. To start with, although the line was crackly and she could barely hear his voice, Van thought he was accusing her of stealing his wife.

His words didn't make much sense. She wondered if she was talking to a lunatic.

'Just because you have no thought for tomorrow,' he shouted, 'it doesn't mean to say that I am sailing in the same boat. It's all very well for you with oodles of cash and grown-up children. It's difficult for me all alone here with Charlotte. Luckily she's a nice child, not that that will last with a mother like the one she's got – or had I should say.' His voice rasped on.

He wanted his wife to return to him. It was all Van's fault. He, Michael, had heard of her infatuation with Johann. It was because of it that Carola had set her cap at the Hun again. She wouldn't have bothered without competition. That was for sure. Carola never wanted anything unless there was some-body else, up in front, wanting it too. The message was, in brief, that if Van would let go of her hold on Johann then Carola would pack it in and return to the burnt-out mountain where she would live in peaceful harmony, happy ever after, with husband and daughter. A likely story.

Van, matching the frenzy of her interlocutor, shouted that her hold over Johann was nothing if not futile; that it didn't exist. She hoped, accordingly, that Carola would soon return to the charred fold.

She lay on the kitchen table, above the hard tiles of the floor.

Baby frogs, transparent green, darted in clumps of iridescent moss, luminous and spongy, clinging to the side of damp bricks. The bricks formed part of a wall, its foundation in a ditch where she sat with her sister, each dreamily shaking a pint-sized milk bottle.

Why was she so distant from her sister? She could have helped. The fault lay with Alice's husband. He had never liked her.

Using a curled-up envelope, they had funnelled crushed aspirins, stolen from the medicine chest, into the milk. Alice had added drops of iodine and juice of deadly nightshade. It was a competition. Which pint of milk would be the first to transform into butter? Losing patience, Alice said 'Don't let's bother. It's bound to have turned by the time it gets there.' On each bottle they glued labels: 'THIS IS NOT POISON'.

Their mother asked them if they needed help. Van, six years old, said 'It's OK. Alice has found his address.' Her respect for Alice knew no bounds. In layers of rags and paper, rationed and rare, they wrapped the clunking bottles. HITLER, THE PALACE, GERMANY, the address dug deep in pencil on the outer wrapping. The two sisters walked briskly over a wide surface of lawn, across a path and through a gate; then over a rickety bridge crossing the ditch in which they had sat, shaking poisoned milk. They were heading for the post office.

Lily Knight, the postmistress, had only one arm. She had been born with two but one had been mangled in a factory accident and amputated high, nearly at the shoulder. The unneeded sleeve, caught by a safety pin, was hitched behind her back. Rough and whiskery, she lived in terror of being raped. Accepting their parcels, she thumped each with a smudgy punch and added the sum they gave her onto the family account. On the way home they found their mother cross-legged on the lawn making a daisy chain. She didn't tell them that she kept a revolver by her bed for fear of parachutists. Their father was away at war.

Van's energy came in fits and starts. It was imposssible to predict when it was going to invade or desert her. What if she had given birth to triplets? Spina-bifida triplets with a hole in each heart. She would have slapped a paternity suit on Johann.

Sometimes their mother would go to London, richly dressed in jewellery and a large hat, caught up in a veil. They would wait for her to return at the bridge near the bus stop; throw themselves into her arms and beg to know how she was.

'Well. Just a little tired.' She must have looked unique sitting on the bus beside highly painted young ladies, padded shoulders, bursting buttons and short tight skirts.

Equivocally she would tell them of her day trip, preferring to hear how they had spent their time. They learnt their lessons at home by post, in touch with an organised education board, petrol being scarce and schools far away. PNEU it was called. Van couldn't remember what this stood for. Alice read a letter that she saw in the library. It was written in a spiky hand.

Not unlike Johann's.

'Sybil dear. I dreamed last night that I lunched with the Queen. How infinitely preferable was yesterday's reality.'

When taxed with it their mother laughed. 'He's a silly old geezer,' she said.

At a certain moment Van had taken to wetting her bed.

The memory of it clouded her rapture as she lay on the kitchen table.

Whatever efforts went into planning the nights before her, it became unavoidable. She would wake early and lie still, screwing her face and praying 'Please God. Please say that I didn't do it last night.' Occasionally her prayers were answered but, more often than not, she suffered warm wetness beneath her. On the bed, now prepared, equipped with rubber sheeting, her mother sang to her. A silly song ending 'Vanessa will go to sleep' on a trill. They gave each other butterfly kisses, using eyelashes. Enclosing her, her mother whispered, 'Goodnight my petkin wetkin.' Van bellowed. It was cruel. 'Good God,' her mother cried, 'I meant pie-kin dry-kin. Silly little fungus. You know that's what I meant.' There was always a joke.

Overnight things changed. They became a dormitory. The Queen Anne house was singled out, as were many, to harbour a contingent of evacuees. Children, victims of the blitz, arrived by coach, twenty-five of them, many rife with ring-worm, under the banner of an institution, Port of London Day Nursery. A matron in uniform accompanied them along with four assistant probationers.

The drawing-room was emptied within the space of a day; heavy curtains were looped out of reach, bringing shutters into play. Chandeliers and pendant lamps were dismantled, leaving naked bulbs. Carpets were rolled up making way for camp beds, low and narrow. Smells of urine, Dettol and fetid clothes replaced the sweetness of polish and flowers.

It was busy and strained. Van's mother supervised the black-out in the evenings. Pulling down funereal blinds to cover windows, now plastered in wide bands of sticky paper to prevent glass fragmenting, splintering into rooms from the blast of exploding land-mines.

Talking to the probationers was enthralling. Their eyes were turned towards a local camp hastily erected for Canadian soldiers, renowned for romancing, chocolate and nylon stockings. The world was full of personalities. Great Aunt Maisie, formal and stingy, driving in a pony trap, lived nearby with Great Uncle Archie. He knitted dishcloths on vast wooden needles like little rolling-pins, and gathered armfuls of stinging nettles for supper. Uncle Archie had a favourite game known as 'stuffy lodgings'. It gave him licence to sit on them. One day he tried to play it when Van was sitting on a gate. It didn't seem fair to play 'stuffy lodgings' out of doors. She warded him off and lost her grip, falling in knee-high nettles, a clump not yet devoured. She climbed out of the clump, her skin red and bumpy. Smarting, she ran to her mother.

'Now he really is a silly old geezer,' she said, not for the first time.

Lunch, squirrel or pigeon, dandelion and nettle leaves, they ate in a dark dining-room along with matron and the probationers. The homeless children ate before the rest.

They looked out to ancient yew-trees and a hilly meadow beyond. The baby, Van's brother, was fed with delicacies, hoarded and hidden from other members of the household. He sat, like a sage, strapped into his chair, gaining weight by the day.

At the head of the table their mother fought to keep the conversation bright. The strain must have been great.

'Too ghastly,' she announced at lunch, 'Fanny Brindle is expecting another baby and she's sold all her clothing coupons.'

'Mum,' Van asked, 'how do you know when you're going to have a baby?'

Now her mother was put to the test. Light of touch, she flew above earthly matters, passing most things off, including her mother-in-law, as 'a fact of life'.

'It's perfectly easy for Fanny. She never isn't.'

They had to sing a round, a complicated one with a rousing chorus, Matron joining in.

Van and Alice spent hours piecing together fragments of a love-letter. It had been sent to one of the probationers by a Canadian who had got 'too fresh' with her. Nanny called them. She was there to look after the baby but would help in all matters now, the house being topsy-turvy.

She was a kleptomaniac but their mother said it really couldn't be helped. One day she took a parcel of their treasured party clothes to Lily Knight at the post office. She was sending them to her niece but Lily smelt a rat and held the parcel up, as she had done with the poison for Hitler. On her day off Nanny went to a mortuary nearby and passed the time laying people out. 'You squeeze out the body juices dear,' she told Van. 'Close the eyes and pop a bit of cotton wool up the nostrils. Then, dear, I fold the arms and sing a verse from "Abide with Me".' Nanny couldn't eat onions. She said they went straight through her.

Joan, the cook, was in tears over the dandelion soup. She was engaged to a butcher, the one who had delivered meat to the house in better times. He was fighting and the letters he wrote were blocked out by security, but for a sentence here and there. She gleaned strength from Jayne, a cartoon character in the *Daily Mirror*, and her dachshund Fritz.

One night Van's mother, tired out, noticed a light in the lavatory next to her daughter's bedroom. A punishable offence. Torn between rousing Van, ordering her to leave her bed to rectify the matter herself, she decided, just this once, to be lenient. The door was open and the light escaping from it capricious, gentle and flickering. Flames, sharp and isolated, licked about the cistern above the lavatory. She stood surrounded by radiant heat. No smoke.

They were all out on the lawn below the stars. All but Joan and Elsie, one of the probationers, who were trapped in the burning wing. How many people the house held. Twenty-five refugees, martialled by matron, filed out in rank in their pyjamas, shy without dressing-gowns. The telephone was out of order. In a flapping silk wrap, Van's mother, head of the house, ran towards the village where the policeman, P.C. Miles, lived in a newly built row of council cottages. She met him on the road and tried to tell him of her plight.

'Funny you should turn up Madam,' he mused. Speaking slowly, he said, 'I was on my way to give you a bit of a wigging. Light's showing at the big house.' Flames appeared from the roof, easily seen above the trees which sheltered the house from the village street. Joan and Elsie were still within. 'By rights I should arrest you.'

She slapped him on the face. 'You cretin. Don't be such a bloody fool. Can't you see the house will be burnt to the ground in a few minutes?' This had the desired effect.

He turned back, accepting now that he must summon the fire-brigade. On the lawn Van hugged the baby, too fat to walk although it should have been possible at that age. One of the firemen fell from the engine as it careered up the drive, knocked off by a low branch. He screeched like a peacock as his arm cracked.

Joan and Elsie, at the back of the house, were rescued by ladder; thrown into sheets by yellow-uniformed heroes. Then it was water. Hoses were unwound and dragged to the stream; sparks shot from chimneys in communal dismay.

Why had she burnt Johann's clothes?

A day later, the burnt-out wing under a flapping tarpaulin, P.C. Miles came to call. He had to make a statement, he said.

Blackout regulations. They had broken the law, showing lights, whatever the extenuating circumstances.

He knew that she would be shaken.

'Not in the least,' she told him. 'I may be lots of things but I'm not shaken.'

'Very well, Madam. I've prepared a statement for you to sign. Thinking you'd be shaken.' She could hardly resist laughing on reading the words he had put into her mouth.

'I was proceeding in the direction of the council cottages in order to inform P.C. Miles that my mansion was ablaze.'

Another brother, on holiday from an evacuated boarding-school, teased them to death. He hid behind an armchair in Nanny's bedroom, jumping up only when her nudity was fully displayed as she tweaked a whisker from above her upper lip, looking in the glass. Their father, on one of his rare wartime visits, walloped him with a leather-soled slipper.

Van, in a rush, pushed her chubby legs hard down into the squelch of Wellington boots, filled with a cluster of baby mice, now one lump of slime.

There had been so many deaths. Neddy, the cat, the rabbit, mice, birds, kittens.

She remembered the doodlebugs. One evening she was sitting beside her mother at the dressing-table as she twisted the roly-poly curls and pinned them into place. Unpinned, her blonde hair hung, heavy, as low as her waist. She started, wary, and made for the window. It wasn't easy to get a clear picture through the strips of paper clinging like fly-traps to the panes. In the distant air the noise of a machine stopped. They could hear the whine of the air-raid siren, housed in the village on the site of an abandoned market garden, starting on its upward wail before reaching a peak and descending. Then they made for the air-raid shelter, a dungeon at the back of the house, across the courtyard from the burnt-out wing, now known as the 'ruin'. The air-raid shelter was the cosiest place in the world, cushioned with mattresses, candles and games.

It reminded Van of her Tuscan house before the bad days of Johann. Bad, bad Johann.

In wet weather the baby's pram, with him in it, stood in the cloakroom under the skylight, surrounded by gas masks. He would have been splintered to death had a land-mine erupted. Nobody had thought to crawl onto the roof with sticky bands of paper.

From time to time their father came home. On one occasion he had grown a moustache. 'Either it goes or I do,' he was told by his wife. He shaved it off before dinner.

Hindustanis had come to the neighbourhood. They would hang over the railings, the garden boundary, and teach Van and Alice to count in Hindustani. Ekki, Dekki, Lordi, Lummyi, as Van remembered it, counting to four. An open truck-load of them drove through the village beside the ditch and along the road, stretching from a gnarled quince tree heavily hung with hard fruit. The truck slowed down and lean brown hands tugged, snatching, mistaking quinces for pears, cramming them into their mouths. Later Van and Alice, walking with their mother on the strewn road, kicked into the ditch the bitten rejects, endowed with scent both bitter and musky, before opening the gate leading into the garden through which they had to pass on their way to church.

Neither Van nor Alice could bend their arms. They wore coats made of tiger skins, stiff as boards. Dejected by the dearth of clothing coupons and powerless in the face of Nanny's purloining, their mother had sent for Lily Knight's daughter, the village seamstress. She was ordered to carve up a mothy rug, a proud trophy of Van's grandfather's game hunting days.

'Serve him right. Frightful old codger,' their mother said as Lily's daughter severed the head from the spread-out skin with a fretsaw.

As the bells chimed they scuttled up the path through the garden laid out on a slope past a hazelnut tree (which Joan called a cob) and nectarines spreading over a south-facing wall. In early summer, low box hedges caged lily of the valley, densely packed. The baby would be left behind, more often than not under the skylight.

Their ·mother, a low-toned chantress with perfect pitch, sang an alto accompaniment to the hymns. Her daughters warbled unseen by the congregation as they perched in a family pew, a loose-box on stilts at the back of the church.

Reverend Bounds conducted the service. Although young, he wore a hearing aid and suffered an impediment in his speech. A clatter, a sort of clank, resounded from his palate only and always at the utterance of the letter K sound, frequently used in matins. Christ, Kingdom, Crown, Cross, Crucifixion. Well groomed, in fleecy white, gleaming dog-collar, he announced from the pulpit. 'This morning my wife presented me with a bouncing baby boy. We are going to call him Christopher.' The boy's name emerged at concert pitch, a pluck on a guitar, deafening and high-falutin'.

'Out of Bounds,' Alice signalled to Van and they howled into their handkerchiefs.

Their mother said, 'Can it, will you? Plug it. You really are silly little gherkins.'

The announcement of Christopher's christening exploded, further pistol shots in the Norman nave, blasting consecrated air.

Van's consciousness twitched. Kimono, Cooking, Kraesel, Carola. Each word a Chinese firework. It came back to her. Hard C. That was the technical term, not the letter K sound.

The Reverend Bounds called the congregation to their knees and entreated them to pray for the clergy. One more firework. 'How selfish he must be asking us to pray for him like that,' Van thought. They walked home, arms linked in spite of the stiffness of the fur encasing them, past a crater in which an unexploded land mine was rumoured to be lodged, despite denials by the Home Guard, then past a spindly windmill, a propeller perched on a rusty frame, a miniature Eiffel Tower. Len, the butcher, was home on leave. Joan had gone to meet him, first promising Van that she would be a bridesmaid when it was all over. Van prayed for the safe arrival of the poisoned butter. That seen to, she would follow Joan, at snail's pace, up the aisle towards the white-robed figure of the Reverend Bounds.

Her mother was in charge of the cooking. She had arranged for a high-hued corned beef hash, in an earthenware pot, to be warmed up by Nanny. Nanny, in terror of finding an onion hidden in the meaty shreds, had sifted the mixture with a long-handled fork, picking at it. It had dried out in Nanny's care and their mother, on her return from church, threw a jug of cold water into the pot.

'That should pulverise it at the very least.'

The earthenware pot was borne into the dining-room where Matron and the probationers, out of uniform on Sunday, waited hungry and unhopeful. Their heroine, Van's mother, tripped and fell, the contents of the pot slopping over as it landed some feet in front of her, a formless pink flow, on a Samarkand rug. She was on her feet and kicking the pot. It spun off, landing at an angle of the room by the china cupboard, trailing a slug-like discharge of corned beef hash behind it.

'That'll fix it,' she said. It wasn't mentioned again. She was firm about this. The debris remained on the floor until lunch was over. An apple per person and a pickled egg. There was a whacking tin of yellow powder on the kitchen shelf, 'scrambled egg powder'. 'Buttered eggs', their mother called it, although there was seldom any butter.

They found some clogs in the dressing-up box. Chiselled from hard wood, there was no give in them. Their mother found them clattering on the flagstones between the dining-room and the kitchen.

'Let's learn a dance for when Pop gets back.'

She sat, curls over the piano keys, ringed fingers moving fast as her daughters rehearsed, their feet in excruciating pain, a speedy clog dance.

'By the side of the Zuider Zee', it was called. They wore bunchy skirts and dish-cloths, knotted to form flaps over their ears. The dance ended on a twist and the line 'There my Dutchie girl waits for me, only me.' They made a false fall, feet and bunchy skirts in the air. It was good. Their mother liked it.

Their father returned, handsome and remote. The dance was set up for him to watch in the music room. Sofas were pushed back against walls and the rug was rolled up. A vast cylinder.

A blown-up version of Johann's air-mail editions.

Their father sat next to matron. Joan and Nanny were called in. The probationers were also present. They began. Two figures in pinching clogs danced to their mother's music unsmiling and resolute. As it progressed they accelerated, adding laxity to the performance. The pianist speeded up, excited. They were well away. Their father rose and made for the door.

'A couple of elephants,' he said as he turned the handle.

Matron muttered 'Isn't he cruel?'

Alice and Van laughed themselves nearly to death. Their mother had tears of mirth in her eyes.

'Isn't he priceless?' she said.

# Chapter
## VIII

If only Johann hadn't grown a moustache. It was as if he knew, had discovered, a method of further torment.

Not far from Rockingbourne there was an antiquarian bookshop specialising in botany and birds. Uncle Jim knew the proprietor. They would pay the shop a visit; give Van a treat. Uncle Jim parked his car, methodically, on the side of the road opposite the shop, higher up the hill. He didn't lock it. 'No need in a small place like this.'

It was a nice shop. The books were well set out and it was easy to find your way around. At once her uncle was absorbed, but Van found it hard to settle, her finger hurting as it did. She didn't want to spoil Uncle Jim's fun but, equally, she couldn't concentrate; couldn't go on. Now her whole arm was aching, at any rate as far as she could judge, from the elbow down. The pain was impossible to isolate. Uncle Jim, up two rungs of the library steps, called to her. 'I won't be long, darling. You go to the car. You look mouldy. Cuddle up in the back. You'll find a rug and there's a cushion I use for my back.' Grateful, she took his advice and tucked the rug around her on the back seat; knees bent and head jammed into the cushion pressed against the window. It wasn't easy with the pain shooting up her arm but she managed it somehow, flipping her shoes off and lighting a cigarette. After ten minutes the handle of the door rattled; the one beside the driver's seat in front of her. Uncle Jim with a purchase? No. A pale old face looked into the back. It was a man's face, gaunt and crinkled. The owner of it wore a dog-collar, stiff and white.

'Can I help you?' he had a kind voice.

'Oh. Please.' She was touched, happy.

'Can I take you somewhere?'

'No. I'd rather stay here please.'

'Very well.' He was gentle. 'But there's a problem. This is my car.'

Van had made herself so very much at home, snug in the rug and smoking furiously, shoes on the floor. It was flabbergasting. She looked behind her and she could see Uncle Jim waiting, consternation on his face, at the wheel of his car a few yards back.

She cried as the vicar helped her out and handed her over to Uncle Jim. Their cars were different colours; different brands.

Uncle Jim said, 'Darling, I think you should be helped. Of course you're not mad but you're very unhappy and it might do you good to talk to an impartial listener. I'm no use. I could strangle the kraut with my bare hands.' Kindly he was telling her that she was disturbed, in trouble of the sort no friend could handle. He made enquiries and sent her the address of a psychiatrist in Harley Street. 'I've heard he's the tops, darling. I'm sure you'll only need one visit. Please go. I'll pay.' She promised she would, her fear of Johann all consuming. It would be the true end. Once and for all.

In the waiting room she wondered how to present the tale. She cried as she waited. A soothing voice and a hand on her arm. The voice was telling her that the doctor was behind schedule. He would have to keep her waiting, and would she like a cup of coffee? She said 'yes' to the coffee and told the nurse, politely, that it didn't matter. She had all the time in the world. Now all she wanted was to be normal.

A picture of the doctor, well behind schedule, grew in her thoughts. Would he notice her finger in the holster? Perhaps he would have a moustache, a rusty brown one. Maybe his hair would be black, tinged with white, and his eyes dark and darting. Surely not. He would be old and bent and uninterested in what she had to say. He might tell her that she had behaviour problems or a negative approach; perhaps he would offer her a glass of sherry or tell her to take up knitting.

The soothing nurse told her to go up the two flights of stairs to the consulting room. Demurely she faced him, a boy in a smart blue suit. Clean-shaven, he held out his hand and then withdrew it, sympathetically, when he noticed the leather finger sticking up like a mouldy banana. They sat facing each other, across a desk. His eyes were black but they didn't dart. They looked humorously at her.

'I'm afraid I don't know why you're here. I've had no letter about you. No introduction. Nothing. You'd better start telling me. Say what you feel like.'

It didn't bother her. She liked him and, anyway, she longed to talk. Firstly she told him about Neddy and the death at the kennels. It took a bit of time but he didn't mind. He was interested and laughed aloud once or twice, amused by her descriptive powers. He guided her backwards and the tale emerged. She stopped. It had taken her an hour and a half. The doctor, who had listened keenly, stood up and shouted, 'My God. What a rotter. I'm glad you burnt his clothes.'

'I thought you were supposed to be dispassionate.'

'Not in this case. Nobody will ever get the better of him. He's the one who should be sitting here. Not you. Not that I could do much for him. Nothing at all, I daresay.'

'So I'm not mad? What about my acts of destruction and violence?'

'Wonderful, simply wonderful. Very positive. It was only a stand. You were selective. You didn't burn books or manuscripts which you tell me were there. Clothes are replaceable and, from what you say, his were particularly tiresome. I'm surprised you didn't shoot him. You are confused. You think that, because you were capable of one violent act, you might commit several in a variety of contexts. That is ridiculous. You are not going to burn your mother's clothes or open the letters of your friends. You are not going to rip pubic hairs from the nearest policeman. Not mad at all. The very reverse. Had you told me that you had merely gone to bed, resignedly, when he didn't turn up, then I might have wondered. Come again, as soon as possible. We will probably only need one more meeting.'

She was glad that he didn't call it a 'session'.

'We need to explore, just a little, how this rotter came to have such a hold over you.' He demonstrated the 'hold' by gripping two of his fingers together. When she left he offered her his left hand to shake. His stars were in the ascendant, dominating her direction. The words 'what a rotter' and 'I wonder you didn't shoot him' cheered her. The clamp lifted from around her temples and it came to her, very clearly, that she would never see Johann again. Could he have been a magician, this boy, hardly older than Melissa?

'A human condition', he had called it. Not insanity or derangement. Moreover it was curable and he was going to help her. During the few days between her visits – 'meetings' – she seemed to rise like Lazarus from her sick bed. Snowdrops were in flower. There was a backlog of housekeeping which she returned to with rediscovered will. Melissa said, 'We're glad to have you back Mum. You have been away an awfully long time.' So she had. A year and a half under a spell.

A letter came from Johann. It was the morning of her second appointment with Dr Chapel. He sought a reconciliation and offered a number of excuses for past behaviour. 'I've been thinking of you a good deal, and in particular two things. One is the appalling way I behaved. It may seem absurd to you if I say it, but it is only becoming absolutely clear to me now – clearer with every day. The other thing is that it wasn't simply, entirely my fault in plain terms – my behaviour was because I, too, was a victim of circumstances, and I was out of control with everything around me out of control too. I have to believe this to stay sane. I hope you believe it too. But it is your suffering I think about more. I am absolutely longing to see you . . . ' What luck she was going to Harley Street. On an ordinary day she would have taken to her bed, crippled with indecision, after a letter like that. Then she would have answered it or rung him up, anything to keep herself alive in his consciousness.

She showed it to Dr Chapel.

'Why did you open it?' he asked. 'You could have burnt it,

unopened. You are, after all, rather good at that sort of thing.'
He looked at her, smiling.

'Curiosity, perhaps.'

'Victim of circumstances, my foot! Victim of brutal selfishness is nearer the truth. He's dying you know. Dying. Soon he will be dead.'

'Literally or metaphorically?' She was alarmed.

'It doesn't much matter.'

The doctor said that he had given her much thought. He didn't say 'her case'. The complexities of her life before meeting the 'rotter' had been dealt with efficiently, he said. Capably and courageously.

'Your involvement with this man is the first thing to have knocked you sideways. This tells me a great deal about him. Wow! He'd be an interesting case, not, as I told you before, that I could do much with him. There are still such things as bad characters, you know.'

'Can I come and see you again?'

'Not for the present. My door is always open to you. My clinical diagnosis, if you want one, is this. You are a very emotional woman and a very passionate one. You handled this affair badly but that doesn't mean you are unbalanced. You fell for him. Decent women fall for rotters from time to time. The same in reverse. Now it is over. Dead. If you cling on it will be destructive and that would cause problems, self-disgust and so on. I should, now, like you to turn the whole episode upside down in your mind and salvage what was good in it. Turn it to good account. Come back if you need help but, meanwhile, it will do you no good to talk about it either to me or to anyone else.'

She rose, strengthened, and held out her left hand for him to shake. As their hands met he looked at her enquiringly. 'You're not off to meet him for lunch are you?' The trivial joke held her, entranced, for weeks to come. It was sad that she was not going to see him again but his words remained with her and, when low, she pictured him rising, enraged, from his desk and shouting 'rotter'.

# *Chapter*
## IX

It was summer. One hundred and one per cent extricated, Van delighted in her immunity. She had rediscovered the power of standing alone. Johann was very small: Tom Thumb. She could have slipped him into a box, snapping the lid; or into a sponge bag, zipping it tight.

Her niece, sister of the one who had married in Cornwall the autumn before, came of age. Pretty as paint, the eighteen-year- old despatched bundles of invitations. Family and friends were asked to celebrate in a leafy London garden.

Van, free again, rid of her burden and back to normal life, was delighted to go to her niece's party.

There were guests of all ages. Laura, the friend who had rescued her from Kennington after the discovery of Carola's letter, the 'massive interlect' one, ran up.

'Darling Van. How wonderful to see you. You've changed. You look younger; brighter.'

Laura introduced her to a man. He had been pestering her and was sticking close. She winked as she did it. This one was not to be taken to heart. Wallace Shelton was his name. Van, unaware that she had ever sighted him, turned her head. He was tall and dark, middle-aged, a snazzy dresser. 'We have met before. At the Pathfinders. It was quite an evening. Are they old friends of yours? Janet is a great girl.'

Staring, straight at him, she replied that she remembered nothing of the occasion. Beside a tree, a mulberry bush, stood Greta, self-effacing and shy. There was a ripple in Van's mind but she fenced it off.

There was to be no back-tracking, no relapses. Hiding the twinge in a mental cubby-hole, she looked ingenuously at him.

'It can't have been me.'

'It most certainly was.'

She faltered; then a smart of recognition; a signal of understanding in her eye. She laughed, merry, and ceded.

'Oh dear. It happens so often. That must have been my sister. Poor darling. What has she been up to?'

'It was you.'

'I'm not surprised. Everybody thinks that at first. We're very alike to look at. Twins. We behave differently. That's all. It's confusing.'

Looking at her, searching thoroughly, he saw that he had been wrong. They were different. He should know. He had kissed her juicily enough. This one was bright and strong; sober. The other had been a pushover.

'You're right. For a moment I thought you were pulling my leg. What has become of her, and what's your name?'

'I'm Veronica. My sister's Vanessa. Van, we usually call her.'

'That's right. She was introduced as Van.'

'Poor Van. She's fine really but she gets into terrible pickles, and gets taken for terrible rides. How was she that evening?'

'Well. Fish out of water actually. She spent the evening crying. Crying and drinking. We boys led her on a bit. All good fun. You should look after her.'

It was by chance that she met Johann again. Thanks to his birthday present she was walking down the steps of the London Library. The possibility of bumping into him there had never occurred to her. Although he had assured her that he was a regular visitor, she had distrusted him, never having seen signs of his literary appreciation. It shocked her to see replicas of garments she had burnt. Like hydra's heads they had simply reappeared. Weeds, rooted out of flowerbeds reappear. Lina's scar had paled. Her own finger had mended although it never returned to its original shape.

'Come and have lunch. I've got toothache.' He stuck his thumb in his mouth and began to fish about at the back. For a second she wondered if he was going to make her fish about too. He asked her if she had a clove in her bag for him to chew on.

'Christ Almighty. It must be a nerve. I'm the sick man of Europe. You look wonderful. I miss you, Van. It's a terrible wrench for me not seeing you.'

She thought of Dr Chapel. 'He's dead. Dying. Dead.'

She knew better than to lunch with a dead or dying man, particularly one who had toothache and who was wearing clothes that had been destroyed. Let Veronica lunch with him. Bad Veronica; weak and idle.

The image of the humane-killer, applied to his temple, had long since deserted her and she wished him well. Nothing more. He told her that Carola was back with Michael. 'Expecting another child, I gather.'

He asked her if she would like to go to the theatre with him one evening. Maybe a concert at the Barbican.

'You decide.' She had decided. Vanessa, good Vanessa, would return to the country, serve in the shop, take Winnie to the town; write to James and Henry. Now they could be proud of her.

They kissed goodbye. The moustache had been shaved off and the unborn son, who had hitherto inexorably haunted her, melted back into his body, one composite and ludicrous figure with toothache wearing a check-cloth cap.

The parting had taken Five Rehearsals.